For P...

Strange ... the Park

An Anthology

Bert R. Wells

Best Wishes,

Bert R. Wells

Stranger In The Park first published in 2011 by Bert R Wells

e-mail: wellsbert@rocketmail.com
www.info@granitecaveproductions.com

ISBN 978-0-9569954-0-7

Printed by Print Resources Hertfordshire England
www.printresources.co.uk

Acknowledgments

Creative assistant to Bert R. Wells, Kellie Sisson
With great thanks to Richard Painter & Print Resources

Dedicated to my Beloved father
Frank Richard Wells
Thank you Dad

Frontispiece: *Sol & Luna* by Juliet Asher. © Juliet Asher.

Contents

Priorities

I could be a king,
but I want to know
how to be a man first.

Monet's Morning

Oh, hurtling hillocks!
Thrashing through this
November morning,
XR3 I'd, decked with shades
And Dido's melancholic poetry,
Touching notes, splashing images,
Splashing sun.

Green glass slopes, slope by
And undulate, cuddly.
Great curtains of gold, cloaking,
And I'm choking for a pint,
Staring at Autumn wonder.
Thinking of Monet, money
And freedom.

Hereford beckons! A beacon
To aim for, and the Lady
Folds and moulds the car,
Holding the road like a limpet.
Tyres sweating for grip,
Timeless woven, braided tapestries,
Landscaped.

Melting into the mirrored gold,
Finding peace in beauty, dissolving,
So beautiful, so absorbing,
Swallowed into the womb,
The tomb of nature, unrelenting.
Tears fall unseen in released pain and joy behind
Ray bans.

Tryst of Trust

Sometimes in the darkest hours,
truth seduces to be known.
Hinting at its offerings, when,
two or more share the glimpses
shining salmon silver
on twilight bowers.

Do we touch then, in subtle
and unspoken ways?
Coming closer, naturally, dancing
beside the shadows of thoughts -
dreamt, hidden; unleashed unwittingly
before the end of such sought after days.

Dusk sweet, dusk night
approaches, and parting
softly shares its frozen whisper.
Soft, caught, found and imagined
captures a kiss, and leaves
two souls quietly smarting.

What wincing wounds are these,
tripping squaddie booted
over friendship's fields?
Tingling memories that cry, don't!
Become, be one, sleep easy,
let truth and friendship appease.

Have I seen correctly, the present image yonder?
As I hold it in layered dreams and dead days.
Shall I begin to flounder, while
I hang on to old flames and pathways trod?
I will but hold the door of mind open
and, leave my soul to ponder.

Cherry Trees

The veggie juice
ran rivulets down
our chins,

while the moon
danced circles
in our eyes.

Marlene Dietrich
came to mind,
though I wouldn't

sing the words.
The cool night air
blossomed on our

cheeks, while a full
moon smiled over
Washington,

Like the Japanese
trees around the
lake, crowning.

Demons

I could have loved you better,
if only I'd known how.
I know my love was lacking,
failing, failed somehow.
Still waters run deep they say,
then love must surely be still.
Calm and peaceful,
all embracing, love that
would wish no ill.

You, were the Ariadne of my
Minotaur mind.
Into the maze of darkness,
I fell and wandered blind,
like Milton's 'Eyeless In Gaza',
my own persecutors I couldn't see,
but those enemies of my sanity,
all belonged to me.

Ankomst – (Arrival)

I arrive on the straining back of a stormy sea,
leaving raging white foaming white horses,
gasping for air. From the united green isle over
blue grey waters to a land of living tales and
caterpillar hills, writhing and turning back
on themselves, sine wave like, belt like,
across and tucking in neatly the black brown
jersey of the october landscape. As I leave the
snorting stallions of the sea, I also discharge
my thoughts.

At once seeking sure ground, I am met with
challenge, the gauntlet of truth tossed into my
shadow. The dark veil draws open, slowly,
purposefully, like a Viking's helmet raised
briefly, to scan the field before the ensuing
battle. Then firmly slammed down tight, the
struggle ensues. Sunlight blinks through the
eye-holes, casts light upon dark areas, hidden
beneath layers of dreams. I squirm worm like
before the seeking rays, and the stone of my
ignorance is turned over, the murky underside,
cold and damp is forced to receive the fire of
the solar lamp.

This lamp does not go off. For he that throws
the switch never sleeps, is no living mortal and
bears no flesh but mine, for my own suffering,
and in the incessant light the crooked inhabitants
of my flawed mind, rise before me in a crescendo
of maggot moving resistance. Unwittingly prostrate
before lordly doves, who, in their pure white
unflecked feather down armour, survey the mass,
pulling only ripest parasites from their rotting haven.
Infant shadows are spared the charge of the light

brigade. Seedling of the unending uroberous of stress,
conflict and growth, 'til only virgin mind remains.

Here, even a walk home becomes a challenge.
At night, it is no quick stroll up the high street,
but a meandering up and downing, roundabouting
confrontation with north winds from the russian
steppes, that dance razor like upon southern grown
cheeks. From here, you can hear Thor, bellowing from
Asguard. He has his own windphone, connected to
Iddrasyl. And all the trees that guard and line the
landscape, seem bent with the weight of Thor's hammer
hanging from every branch, or bowed with old age
as the mighty voice hurls its icy breath, and gnarls
even the strongest aborific child. Suddenly, you stop.
Ears reach to the woods, the tinkling, singing
chimes and falling tunes of the thawing icicles,
drop in chordal obedience to the wind. They play
the battle song eerily, within a hidden silence
throughout this full mooned thinly cloaked night.

Where am I, while this battle rages? Me? I sleep,
yes, sleep, not too deep behind a fag paper thin
blindfold, wrapped loosely tied, half heartedly
optimistic through shying eyes, that know better.
My blankest of warmth and feigned unknowing,
 are meaningless buffoonery, mixed with cops and
robber drives into a green domed city, that's not
expecting this dance with an unknown end. Pretty
distractions talk and become walking telephone
numbers, giving off the scent of liberated promise.
And Jack the lad still sleeps, dishing out lucid
wit and worse, from a pickled mind steeped in the
brew of warriors, capped with credit card glory.
Under Milkwood falls from our lips, and is more
awake than we. Leaving the serving hatch of the
mind, laughing raucous my friend and I, he drunk

on Danish girls and depression, while I fly high
on booze and ribaldry, slashing and splashing a
walk, full shod in and around the fountain,
fumbling for car keys to embark on a fools errand.
The odds are loaded with leaded dice, and death
hovers expectant.

I Am

I am taller than the day is long,
and older than the first Sequoia
that ever bore fruit.

From my wisdom came the owl,
from my strength came the lion,
from my love came mankind.

I am but one life through
eternity, and sojourn in this
vehicle for a while.

My consciousness talks
to me of yesteryears,

and by the light that shines
from my eyes, all can see
the present for years to come.

I am taller than the day is long,
and older than the first Sequoia
that ever bore fruit.

No Cake Thanks.

The candles flamed six in a circle,
He blew them all out in one.
Grinning, smiling faces made rounded
By the table framed light.
Happiness and a unity barely remembered,
Equally forgotten like breathing.
The heart expands with inclusion,
His mother says time for bed,
And in our suited goodbyes,
A space emerges, waiting,
We are acquainted, aloneness
Mastered, because my dad's
A soldier. And I don't know
When he's coming home.

Unbidden Tenant

As I shook the shackles
and images of dreams away from me,
I awoke, only to find myself
in another dream.

Inside this circular stone
tower, I pad my way round
the wooden board-walk, raising
thrusty lingering clouds of dust.

All is silent as sadness and as
calm as understanding, and while
I hear not a sound, I hear all,
for there is no thing to be heard.

Light shines off the grey stones,
reflecting a comforting source
from who knows where. In this light,

the shadows of an alcove emerge.
From out of the dark belly,
glides a huge white figure,
an owl of gigantic proportions,
it lands feather light, beside me.

Dwarfed by this startling presence,
I am not afraid and cause no fear
in it. An unruffled flight of power
and strength, and yet, so embracing.

In the continuing peace and calm,
I wonder why my dubious company
is sought. I watch the owl,
the owl watches me,

with eyes as deep and dark as a
coal mine and as large as soup
bowls. Within the eternity that
was the moment, I realize

what it is, the owl has come
to say. In image and thought;
the language of the Soul,
I hear words so sweet that
tears fight to break out.
'Through years of misery,
you've sought me, for many
an evening you've grieved for me.

Why then, have you not
sought me here? In all the
years waited, I've waited.
When I was behind you,

you drove me away. Now that
we've met, what is it?' My heart

stopped as it all became clear.
All I'd sought before and held

as dear, came to nothing.
And that which has always
been within me, I chose to fear.
Now, tired of waiting, my Self

chases me. Would that I had
but an ounce of its patience.

Some Kind Of Christmas For Raithe

Raithe woke up freezing, his body shivering beneath the frozen quilt. The battered old traveling clock on the window sill said seven thirty. 'So, it's night time already', he thought. Raithe hadn't slept much, he found it too difficult to sleep when he was starving, and he hadn't eaten a thing since Sunday last. It was Sunday again, a week later. Despite the hallucinations he was suffering through lack of food, warmth and sleep, he'd managed to keep the track of days on a calender nailed to the wall beside his bed. It was one his mother had sent him last year and had beautiful views of the Scottish Highlands. It's an old Scottish tradition to send family and friends calenders at Christmas time, in readiness for the New Year. The beautiful views of Scotland's best, cheered up his otherwise lightless, dull bedroom. Raithe hadn't received his new calender, and realised it was late coming when he noticed the day's date. Not only was it Sunday, it was Sunday the twenty fourth of December 1989. 'Some Christmas!', he said out loud, with just a hint of disgust.

He had gone down to England to have a break from his work and at the invitation of a friend, and buoyed by his friend's constant encouragement he'd decided to spend a portion of his life doing what he loved. Raithe loved writing, and he had done just that. He had begun his novel and had written a complete if not perfect anthology of poetry. His friend had written a short story and one poem, fallen in love with a Danish student and promptly disappeared to Scandinavia to delight in domestic bliss. So it had seemed at the time, and within a space of a few short months, Raithe had found himself sharing an old isolated farmhouse with students he had not long met, in the rolling gentle hills of Surrey. Raithe could have never known how terribly different it would all turn out.

Rousing himself, he forced himself upright on the bed and stretched and crossed the room to the little round mirror held in place by three drawing pins on the opposite wall.

Raithe grimaced at his reflection. he looked grotesque, putrid. His eyes had sunk into his skull even more so just recently, dark rings surrounded them, making his naturally dark eyes more so. His pitch black hair and beard had become mangled and straggly, like that of an imagined tramp. The once pale face had now become yellow and blotchy and was peppered with scratch marks, where his now dry and cracking skin itched intolerably. Raithe ran a cold shaky hand lightly over parts of his matted hair, and sighed. He stared into his fiercely shining eyes in the mirror and hoped, hoped to any Gods that might be listening that he hadn't gone mad in his loneliness and hunger. Turning slightly, Raithe cast a sideways glance at his old portable typewriter, stared at it for a few seconds and shook his head. 'It's too cold to write' he said to himself, and he left the grey room muttering incoherently. Limping slightly and stooping at the shoulders, Raithe ignored the cramping pain in his right leg brought on by the cold and damp, and made his way to the kitchen.

He rubbed and clapped his hands together in an attempt to warm them, noticing that his walk too had changed. He no longer walked upright as a Guardsman, but stooped a little round shouldered. The clothes that were bought to kindly hide the now long gone beer belly, hung like sacking on his bent shape as he peered wistfully into the fridge. Of course it was empty, but Raithe looked into it everyday, nonetheless. It was more out of habit, but he couldn't help entertaining just a little hope of a miracle appearance of some tasty morsel. 'No miracles today', he said quietly, then went to the sink and tried the tap for water. Nothing came and Raithe sighed again, though heavier this time with resignation. Straightening, he looked at the glaciated window and the panes graced on the outside with the filigree leaf-like patterns of frost and ice. Quite loudly, he said as though talking to someone else, 'it must be freezing out today'. It sounded like a statement confidently spoken, but there hadn't been anyone else there to talk to for ages. Not since the Norwegian lads had left for home last autumn. 'We're tired of England', Hans had said. 'We're going back to university in

Norway'. Within a week of telling him, they had gone. He'd been alone in the isolated farmhouse for more months than he could or cared to remember. His mind drifted, vague and clear images mixed and fought for prominence in his disturbed memory. His eyes then moved and and he looked beyond the window panes, Raithe shivered slightly and stared out into the blackness of night.

With has hand still resting on the cold steel of the tap, Raithe's mind turned to last winter and remembered a drunken scene, there, in the warm kitchen. Hans and John, the other Norwegian sat at the table with Annette, the Danish wife of the other Brit, Felix, from Sussex. Hans, despite being drunk, played J.J.Cale songs effortlessly on a steel guitar, while leaning back precariously on an old wooden chair. Beside him sat John, seated opposite Annette. The two of them were cradling glasses of wine in hand and debating a point when suddenly Hans, who had apparently overheard most of their conversation, stopped playing his guitar and looked over to Raithe and Felix with a look of amusement about his face. Felix and Raithe who were standing and clowning by the tape player trying to find some J.J.Cale tapes. They stopped their search and turned to look to the others. Raithe looked at Hans, saw his comic expression and watched him hook his thumb to John and Annette. They were still deep in conversation and oblivious to the fact that the music had stopped, and that the other three were watching them. Their conversation had become animated and they took turns topping up each others glasses with the home made red. Raithe and Felix looked at each other and giggled childishly as Felix bent to the cupboard and brought out two blues harps. Handing one to Raithe, Felix turned to Hans, raised his eyes as a signal and waited for Hans to start playing his steel guitar. At each sentence where John emphasised a point, Hans strummed a four note blues riff accompanied by Raithe and Felix on the blues harps.

'...and it doesn't matter who the girl is, it always ends that way...'. Da DA da da. ' I mean, I was drinking when they met me, and so were they...'. Da DA da da.

'...So why do they want to change me? What's that got to do with love?'. Da DA da da. Annette nodded like those dogs seen in the back windows of cars, her face intent, flushed with booze as she topped up the glasses again.

'Does anyone really know what love is, really? Know what I mean?'. Da DA da da, then raucous laughter from the three musicians while John and Annette remained oblivious. Raithe found himself laughing out loud beside the sink and stopped abruptly. The house was cold and quiet again.

Raithe had never managed to find other lodgers and so struggled to get out of rent arrears. As a consequence, the large house became tattier and even began to smell unlived in. What was worse, the staleness of the building echoed his own inner stagnation, his arid lack of creativity. He hadn't written anything of value for weeks. He turned and leaned his back against the sink, he was feeling weaker today, much weaker. 'I must get something to eat', he thought, shaking his head slightly. Feeling suddenly dizzy, he gripped the side of the sink tightly as his body began panting low and deep. More than anything else, all he wanted was to sleep. Just a long deep sleep, but he knew it was impossible. With the increasing hunger, his thoughts at any attempt to sleep became louder and more hurried, giving him no peace at all. At most, in exhaustion the most Raithe could manage was to steal a couple of hours at a stretch, if he was lucky. 'I must get some food', he said quietly and with a frown set upon his features, he limped painfully to the front door.

It was a very cold dark night, and the gravel drive scrunched under Raithe's booted feet, cracking its frozen hard surface. Looking up at the sky, Raithe's eyes saw a vast darkness, highlighted with beacons and a full round moon. Silvery light reflected all over the graceful hilly landscape. His step scraped and clacked onto the frosted tarmacked road, as he limped heavily towards the hamlet of Oak Groves. It was an enchanted view across the hump backed fields. The scattered farmhouses lay squat and dwarfed before the pock marked orb, while the Jewelled blue black heavens draped the horizon. A piercing stillness penetrated the land, and Raithe felt curiously at one with it all, and in a stolen moment of calm thought, his mind latched onto the idea of the Master Jesus. And following that, without particular purpose, he pondered Christmas. Muttering and waving his arms in gestures of explanation, or arguing a point, Raithe half spoke and half thought his two way conversation with his one self.

'Well, I suppose it depends doesn't it, eh? Eh? Eh, eehh, he he..', he giggled childishly. 'Of course, why did he bother, eh?..he he.. good question that, eh?', he said, laughing at some hidden meaning. Then just as quickly, he stopped in his tracks to turn and face the fields, and while his features settled into a serious and commanding aspect, he began to weep the gentle tears of release. He sobbed quietly to himself, but he was thinking about everybody.

'You see, why would he die such an unpoetic death as crucifixion, why would he set himself up for that if it wasn't to show us something? Er, something about love I think it was. Ha! He even loved the bastards that were nailing him up, I mean, what do you think he was, a psycho?'. Raithe's hands left the warm pockets of his trench coat, and his arms took to the air again in a flight of description. To the far left of him, across the glistening landscape, a yellow fog or cloud appeared as though rising from behind the low hills. It was the town lights of Woking, about eight miles away. More and more orange suburbia spread it self across the thin line between light and dark with every step. Just ahead of him, through the sparsely clad trees, the odd twinkling candle could be seen flickering alluringly. Raithe briefly acknowledged the fact and continued with his lonely dissertation. Out of the deep blue, he slapped his thigh heartily.

'Well, Ha HA!', he roared. 'He was either, ha, ha ha, either a cooked up carpenter with a messiah complex or a fully self-realised man. Eh, eh?'. His blazing eyes looked around him as though looking for someone to agree or, disagree with him. 'It's a thought, isn't it?'. His eyes came to rest on the half formed rooftops beyond. 'And you lot?' It was if there was an audience in an auditorium in front of him. Raithe spoke quietly, intimating intimacy, with the palms of his hands turned upwards, he glowered. 'What do you lot really think it's was all about, eh? This Christmas lark? Well,..'. He thrust his hands back in his pockets once more and moved on. 'It's not your fault, is it?' He shrugged his shoulders. 'You only repeat what you were taught, who bought what for who'. His voice sounded almost sad, sorrowful.

Shuffling along with a quickened pace, Raithe began shaking his head slowly in pity. Pity for the people in the next village, pity for the people at home. Pity even for the residents of Woking, in fact pity for the whole human race. He looked back at some of his own Christmases when, with a dodgy motive he too had bought presents for people. Like the construction site managers. He never bought them bottles of whisky to wish them and their families a meaningful spiritual Christmas season. No! that was just to secure further work in the new year. In the warm caverns of his deep pockets, like his mind, his hands fidgeted and squirmed and in a startling moment of clarity, the same mind fixed onto an image of the Master Jesus.

'You wouldn't think he'd come here to teach us about love, would you? What is it they say, in some circles? Yes, that's it. That there's been more blood shed in his name, since he was last known to be on the planet, than in all of man's history. Huh, yeah..', he whispered dreamily. 'Just like that dream'.

Everything was as yet still around him. Only now, he could hear now and then the odd rumble of a lorry in the distance and the occasional call of a solitary pheasant, hidden away in the woods somewhere. A silent night indeed, except that in Raithe's mind, there flashed images of such horror that his face twisted in anxiety and anguish. The dream, he thought. That awful, haunting dream. That face, the Mater's face, contorted in agony. The screams of a man in torment, a God in mortal flesh, burning as only flesh does. Like the branches of freshly cut pine thrown into a fire, the the bark blisters and squares, geometrically painful, mathematical perfection. Fires from the highest and lowest purge him, and never once a look or glance in hatred or in anger. Only pain, The Inquisition, the torture and they didn't realise in all their assumed holiness, who it was they were torturing.

'And in his own name, for God's sake!' Raithe shouted. Then his eyes dashed from left to right in paranoid fear that he was being overheard. But still he wondered, his thoughts running wild like scattering cats. 'But was is just a dream, was it? Or just my loose mind, unhinged? No, perhaps something symbolic, ooh, I just don't know. I'm all confused'. At once he realised he was climbing the gentle hill, with less hurried limping, dragging steps. Now past the pig farm on the left, under the bare spreading branches of a Beech tree. 'Imagine', Raithe thought. 'If he really did come back during the Spanish Inquisition, and we never knew!'

Raithe was in the hamlet now. Fairy lights glistened and twinkled in the windows of the thatched cottages and farmhouses. All the buildings were gathered around a horseshoe pond which lay in the center of the hamlet. At the end of the pond, nearest the road, stood a huge fir tree. As usual for the season, it was decorated with small white lights, and in a gentle sharp wind they flashed intermittently. Looking at their reflection that sprang off from the surface of the now iced water, they reminded Raithe of miniature stars. Tiny solar systems. As though inspecting a company of soldiers, he scrutinised the frost capped sods of turf that surrounded the road. He stopped for a pace and slapped the palm of his hand with a fist, 'of course!' Raithe shouted emphatically. 'Of course he had a purpose. Where are your brains, man?'. His expression changed to a very foolish grin. He chuckled, then strode on. As he moved, he continued his argument with his invisible audience, his arms once more gesticulating. 'What you lot don't understand is, harrumph, he had a reason to go through all that. And what's more, oh yeah, here's the catch, He knew it all from birth. In other words, oh my God, he was conscious of what was to come. It's no good sniggering, you know I'm mad, I know I'm mad. But that doesn't change a thing. Oh no'. His arms were never in one place or at one speed at any given time. His legs, the one forceful and strong, the other, weaker slower and just a little twisted, and that shaggy mane at all times flapping its filthy wisps and matted curls created a grotesque silhouette.

As he emerged from the shadow of one of the bent, gnarled trees that lined the road, Raithe caught sight of his shadow. It gave him a start. He stopped short and stared into it, what he saw reminded him of a distorted vision of Rasputin. Finding it hideous, he snapped out of his trance and walked on with a vengeance, avoiding looking at his dark ethereal companion. His hungry stomach was aching with such a throbbing thud, he could've knocked nails in with it. 'Now then, now then. Where was I? Oh yes, the dream. No, not that. I wasn't there yet, I was..' He whimpered and raised his arms and fists to the heavens in defiance. 'Nooooo', he boomed shaking his fists, 'nooooo!' His bowed his head and sauntered on, muttering. 'No, Christmas isn't about all that at all, not really. He knew this would happen, he must have. I mean..I mean, think about it. To go through all that and then come back again in the inquisition. It was just a dream, only a mad man's dream. Do we celebrate the fact that we murdered a prophet by making the mass for Christ an auction to the highest bidder? And I'm the one who's mad?'

His hands fumbled in his pockets, he was looking for something. He found it, an old pewter pocket watch with ducks and a pond scene of the cover. Flicking it open a face smiled back at him from a small round photo inside the lid. It was a smile that never ceased to warm his heart, and although they found it impossible to live with each other, he knew she had truly loved him and he her. He drew strength from the shining smile and braced himself. He had never asked for food before and the thought of doing so, filled him with mixed emotions. 'You wouldn't have let me get like this, would you?'. With a snap, he closed and pocketed the watch. Her smile had remained infectious, and he grinned lovingly. A little before nine, he thought. Would it not be too late to knock at this hour, and ask for food?

The first door he came to belonged to an old thatched cottage. In the windows burned electric candles, an image Raithe always found odd. From the porch light he could see the green shine of the vinyl door paint, a plain brass knocker stared at him. Without missing a beat, for fear of failing, Raithe knocked loud but courteous. He cringed slightly, it was a little louder than he had intended and the sound floated right across the muffled pond. Behind the door, he could here voices stifled in the inner quiet. Footsteps approached from the inside. The door opened and a portly, short middle aged man looked up at the towering Raithe, and immediately stepped back a pace. Raithe tried to smile politely as he said, 'excuse me Sir. I'm sorry to disturb you at this time of night, only I wondered if you might have some spare vegetables, or perhaps a piece of bread?' The man's lower jaw dropped, leaving his mouth agape. The man shook his head slowly, in disbelief.

'What!?' He demanded, while staring at Raithe in affront.

'What in all the world do you mean by knocking at my door at this time of night? Eh? Speak up man!'

'You see', Raithe began reluctantly. 'I have been expecting a parcel from home, only it hasn't arrived. I was wondering if you had a spare vegetables, or, you know, something to eat'.

'Oh, good heavens. Hum no, no. I'm afraid we er don't have anything. Goodnight!'. The man disappeared as the door shut firmly.

A little dazed, Raithe stared at the door for some seconds quite motionless. The snow had begun to fall again. Thick gently descending flakes, heavily they began settling into a lush mat on the frozen pond and the banks.

'Perhaps I mumbled too much', he mused. He took up his pace again as he shuffled toward the next cottage. It too was thatched and resplendent in Christmas lighted windows, with a holly wreath around the central lion's head brass knocker. A Father Christmas red painted door shone in the oak frame, bent with wind and time. On the jamb was an electronic bell button and beside it, a small dished brass bell. It hung on a black leather boot lace. Raithe chose the bell, it tinkled delightfully and reminded him of meditation bells. It made him smile, and he was milling still when the door slowly opened inward. It stopped about a quarter of the way, Raithe was surprised to see a young girl of about five or six, half hid by the door looking out and up to the strange man. Her bright sapphire eyes framed in heart shaped lush red hair, her arm clasped around a rag doll. The colour of her red frock matched the door. Fleetingly, Raithe absurdly wondered if that was intentional. The thought also flashed across his mind that perhaps, it was a little too late at night for such a young child to be up. Especially on Christmas Eve. The girl didn't move, she just stood there, looking. Not wishing to frighten the little girl, Raithe spoke gently.

'Is your mummy or your daddy home?' The little girl nodded, and stuck her free thumb into her mouth behind her cheek. 'Can I speak to one of them, please?' Her beautiful eyes never left Raithe's face and it occurred to him that he probably looked frightful to her. He smiled gently at her and then heard..., 'who is it?'

It was a woman's voice shrieking from the bowels of the cottage. Quickly following the shout, a heavy footfall brought a large auburn haired woman to the door. 'Oh!', she exclaimed and pulled the young girl inside behind her.

'Yes, what do you want?' she asked pompously, disdainfully raising her nose to the air. 'I'm sorry to disturb you at this time of night, madame. I wondered if you might have some spare vegetables, or some bread that you don't need. Only, I've been waiting for a parcel, it just hasn't arrived'. The lady's face became embarrassed. Raithe began again, slowly. 'I wondered if you might have some spare..'. Before he could finish, a tall thin man with a hook nose and a bald head, thrust his beaked face over the woman's shoulder.

'What the devil is going on! Do you know what time it is? Be off with you, go on. Damned cheek!' The man was clearly very angry and indignant at being so disturbed. Raithe watched the woman speak quietly to the man. 'Oh! Food is it? At this hour', the man growled. This time the woman tugged at the man's sleeve, she craned her neck to his ear and whispered. Beak face remained indignant, 'no I wont hear of it dear. If he gets it once he'll only come asking for more. Besides..;, he glared at Raithe. 'We don't even know who he is'. Raithe interrupted.

'If I may explain, please. I only live up the road in Christina's Grove, you know, the isolated farmhouse on the brow of the hill. I really wouldn't bother you, only... '.

'Only you thought you'd try your luck here, did you?' The man said with a slicing sneer.

'Close the doors and take Heather in with you', the man barked at his wife. Raithe smiled at the little girl as she was tugged back. Her eyes met his and lit up, blue on blue.

'Now young man', beak face continued righteously. 'I suggest you go back to Cristine's whatever it is, and stay there. Or I'll have the police onto you for being a nuisance. And a bloody nuisance you are too, on Christmas Eve of all nights. Honest folk are at home on Christmas Eve. Away with you!'

The irony wasn't wasted on Raithe. The door had slammed with a serious thud and had jarred him. But he remembered the little girl's eyes and her smile and he was warm again, if only in heart. As he stood outside the cottage, his back to the red angry door, a snowflake about the the size of a fifty pence piece landed thickly on the bridge of his nose. It melted almost immediately, and ran in two rivulets down both sides of Raithe's face. With a knotted brow and a pouting lip, Raithe moved ungracefully to the bench by the pond.

Everything was covered in thick snow and Raithe had to scrape a space clear to sit. Behind him, the huge Christmas tree rustled slightly, its wispy shadow dancing like fairies before of him on the snow. He was freezing to the bone. His breath came hard, the freezing air biting the back of his throat, while beneath his thick coat his body shook tensely. With sudden realisation, Raithe discovered that he could hardly feel nor hear, the beat of his heart. He didn't brood on it though.

Instead, he thought about Christmas again. 'It has become an auction', he said softly. 'We've lost it. We've really lost it. Or is it, that I have lost it? I'm outnumbered, it must be me'.

He had almost thought himself into morosity, when he checked himself and instead he took a good look around the pond. What could now be seen of it, that is. It was all white and soft everywhere, all the sharp edges rounded off, silence over all and all the birds still. The pond now, was almost untraceable. The thickness of the snow drifts had practically leveled it off with its banks. The buildings and houses around the pond took on an almost ghostly appearance, subdued, as if their solid structures had become atomised. Their corners were not so pronounced, and yet at the same time the whole picture being forced sharp by the spotlight moon and the footlight stars of the great heavenly stage behind. Mind blowing! So vast it's unthinkable, he muttered.

Calling himself from his reverie, Raithe contemplated trying his luck with the one remaining cottage that shed light. He really didn't want to. He shrugged his snow capped shoulders and with stiffness, rose and moved around the pond to the last house. 'One more try', he said. As he walked he began to notice how his limp had become worse, weakened by cold. What frightened him a little was when he knew he couldn't feel anything at all in his feet. He didn't brood on that either, he kept walking, his tracks crushing the snow until he stopped at the door of the house upon which his hopes were pinned.

The wreath on this door was much more pleasing than the other wreaths he'd seen. The silver knocker was shaped into two fish, top and tailing. Raithe had seen that image before, he couldn't place where though. The wreath that hung from it was made of straw and turned and twisted into the shape of an encircled cross. Two Royal Blue coloured ribbons trailed graciously, the vision touched him. In the moonlight, it shone.

As inviting as the cottage was, Raithe felt a reluctance to pursue his errand. Something held him back, he knew not what. Twice he'd walked away a few steps and walked back with raised hand, to knock. Twice he turned away. He turned away a third time and went and perched himself on a snow covered tree stump. He didn't bother to remove the snow, he sat there in a flummox. He looked at the cottage again, there was a glow from within, perhaps from a lamp or a candle. Who could tell? It emanated warmth, invitation. 'I'm too tired', Raithe told himself. 'I'll try again in a moment or two. Can't give up on everyone just because of a few'.

In the intense cold, it seemed as though his thoughts had thickened somehow, moving slower, clearer. He knew he was numb, he knew he was clear in mind, clearer than he'd been for ages. Clarity had returned, no longer a lost possession, but a treasure. He glanced again at the cottage, he thought he saw a light glow around the place. Raithe decided he was hallucinating again. It looked so comforting and embracing, but his rational mind kept interrupting him, telling him of the stark cottage by a frozen pond in the middle of nowhere.

The decorated tree beckoned to him and drew his attention from the cottage with its gently gyrating branches. It reminded him of a Hindu goddess. Before he knew it, Raithe had risen above his pain and he held his gaze on the tree and the silver star that topped it. It really was a thing of beauty. He was so touched that he became sorrowful. He didn't know why, he didn't want to be sorrowful. Then he blurted out, 'you must have known we'd take forever to listen to you when they nailed you up'.

The tree calmed him. 'That's love for mankind alright. That's...Patience!' Raithe began praying, something he hadn't done in years. He didn't think about it, he just did it. Billowing clouds of breath formed as he mouthed the words to himself, finishing with..'Forgive us our sins, for we know not what we do'. So absorbed in his prayer was he, that he nearly leapt out of his skin when he felt a light tap on his shoulder. 'Don't be alarmed friend', said a kind voice. 'I saw you sitting here and thought you might like some company'. The stranger was tall and spoke very gently, the long hair and full dark beard highlighted his eyes. In Raithe's stammering mind they beamed gentleness, a kindness he'd never known. And yet, there he stood looking about the same age as Raithe, thirty two-ish, not dressed much better either. Although the strangers clothes were old, they were also spotless. The stranger crouched down beside Raithe. Raithe looked at him puzzled.

'I thought I was the only nutter to come out on a night like this', said Raithe quietly.

'Ah well, it is Christmas after all', spoke the stranger. Raithe didn't understand the reply at all, but said nothing. It was then he noticed that the man wasn't actually quite dressed like he, for the man wasn't wearing a coat or anything against the cold. He thought the man must have been freezing. He was going to mention it, but decided against it.

'It's no more strange for me to be out dressed like this, as it is for you to be out at all'. The stranger smiled as he said this. How did he know I was going to say that, Raithe wondered. He must have read my thoughts.

'I did. But let's not worry about that now. How would you like to come into the house and have some bread and soup with me. It's simmering now, as we speak'. Raithe was dumbfounded, his staring face expressionless.

'I live in that cottage behind us', the man said.

'Funny, I was debating whether to knock or not on your door'.

'I know, that's why I came out to you. You did knock, you knocked with your heart'. Again Raithe was left dumbed and gaping, he felt like an idiot.

'It was your selfless plea that commanded me to come. Shall we go in out of the cold?' There was something that was familiar about the man. His frozen thoughts had become sluggish, but he never forgot a face. He then convinced himself that he'd seen the man when out walking the lanes. Whether the man was familiar or not, Raithe still couldn't figure the man out. His talk was a bit way out, a little unsettling. Leaving his thoughts behind him, Raithe rose stiffly to his feet with the welcoming thought of a steaming bowl of broth in front of him. With the helping arm of the stranger, Raithe walked side by side with the man to the cottage.

Once in side, the man led Raithe to a wooden slat bench.

Beside it, a cheery log fire in a brick hearth. Across the room a tall slim, black stove added to the heat and on its top, a cast iron pot simmered. The stranger ladled out two bowlfuls and passing one to Raithe, sat on the bench opposite.

'Here, take this. You'll feel a lot better with that inside you'. The man smiled again, childlike almost. Raithe struggled with the bowl, he was very weak, so his new friend instinctively helped him. Raithe's hands cupped the wooden bowl gratefully. As a wave of embracing unknown love started to roll through Raithe, the stranger said quietly, 'by the way, you were right about that dream last year. I did come back'. Raithe looked up through the soup steam at the man, his eyes welled up in pools. In a whisper, he said, 'that's where I'd seen you before'.

On Christmas morning, the next day a little girl went out to play in the snow on her new sled. It was still snowing lightly and not too cold to test her best Christmas present ever. She had gone all round the horseshoe shape, running and pushing herself into a gentle slide at least twice. When she was about to set off for a third run, her eye caught something that she hadn't noticed before. The little girl looked at it for a few moments quite definite that it wasn't there yesterday. At first, it looked like a tree stump covered in snow. Drawing up close to it however, to her shock and surprise she saw something else. Sitting stiff on the half tree stump, was the funny man who came to the house for food, last night. The man with the nice smile, she remembered. At first the little girl named Heather, thought he was just sleeping, but when she looked into his open eyes they were unmoving. For some reason, she wasn't shocked. Wasn't shocked at all, she had only wondered why he'd stayed out there all night. And why were his hands cupped? It looked as though they'd been holding something, but now they were frozen. Then she saw that he was smiling, blissfully smiling. Slowly, the girl moved away from the man, but couldn't help glancing back at him, curious. He hadn't moved, not a bit. He just sat there, frozen and smiling at something straight in front of him.

Non Starter

I wish I could write like that.
Simple words that say enough
to express the depths and
heights in a single line.
Not to wallow in self pity,
nor lie beneath your feet,
waiting for a reaching hand.

The hand made of sand,
a glimpsing heart of colour,
the mind a convoluting spiral
where a heart once belonged.
Crushed beyond recognition,
fighting for recognition
when your truths are
made of glass.

I'd have loved to love you,
but it's power you crave.
There is freedom in truth,
but the cost is dear;
no false love is worth this.
I've no pain to justify
your freeze dried tears.

There should be a chorus of love,
that rhymes and sings.
I sung once, before you stopped,
but having never started;
an old car in the yard
going nowhere, flat tyres
old and crumbly, worn out
treads instead.

Nonetheless

I have the ambition to pee,
she said.
I have the ambition to
kiss you from your toes
to your head
and all the interesting
bits in between,
I said.

May I have your dream?
I asked.
Last night you breathed
in music and painted
the dark with scent.
Only if you kiss me on the
nose first; winking alluringly
as she barked.

Then, tell me about union,
talk to me of love,
then if I fail to meet you,
fail to greet you,
kiss me anyway and don't
desert me when I struggle,
when I try to balance
what you give me from above.

Because, I love you
imperfectly,
but love you nonetheless.

Doors of Stone

Points of infinity,
the doors we choose not to
open, lie at the center
of our hearts.

Sitting in the woods,
with only the trees for company,
I contemplate the doorways
within their initiate hearts.

Reaching for the heavens,
their source is my source,
but they reach higher than I,
and I sit lowly in their shade.

The trees green and sunlit
mottled brown, desire only
to be trees. Why then do I
not desire that which I am?

Points of infinity,
the doors I choose not
to open, lie at the centre of my
heart, and like the roots of these same trees,

my heart is surrounded by stones.

Silent Vigils

Walking through hidden sacred groves,
old Oaks glorify the path once trod
by the ancients.
Stillness lies in the approaching dusk,
Oak leaves whispering to
a gentle breeze,
as birds chorus quietly, respecting
Holy ground.
Dusk becomes night, cool;
cool as the stone cross
I've just found.
I touch the Celtic patterns
wrought by predecessors
of my own craft.
They eye us still, still
here, guarding, watching,
awaiting
the Romans return.
Their Celtic energy lives
in this stone; the weathered
Oaks meditate
upon it as witnessed by a
shooting star, precipitated
over Glamis's
peak, peering; the Priestess
ensouled by fire to meet my
homecoming.
Confirmation in white heat
of a history I never forgot,
even when
I never knew. A fire returning,
a borrowed sacred flame lent
to me
a long, long time ago. An Amethyst
gowned priestess transferred

the secret
at the slow death of our king,
and now it was home
in these
mountain glens once more. I look
to my brothers' return, reclaiming
their truth
to make this island bristle again.
The Romans never won; they say
I too
was Roman once, a blight to my own.
But the Celts have always been here.
Brothers!
Come home! The Holy
Line remains unbroken.

For A Free Lioness

If I stood before you
like the sun,
or brought you the moon's rays
to reflect off your cheeks,
would you bring your femininity
and grace of form closer to me?

To stand within the light of your eyes,
your gaze is enough
to bring harmony to a soul
sometimes troubled with
self-doubt; though paradoxically
contentment reigns.

The heart of a poet, builder
can also beat with joy,
having met a rainbow incarnate.

Strapling

His fearlessness plunges him forward,
lion brave before men twice his age
as he challenges their carnal knowledge,
cock-sure references to his prowess
and manhood,
all of sixteen.

The men shake their heads, pitying.
His childlike wonder, their bemused boredom.
Finding his way to the right end
of a tape measure, he would dare
try to belittle the boss, slighting
worldly knowledge as old.

I wuz doin' it in Baghdad before
you wuz in ya dad's bag, yungun!'
The youthful grin turns pinky red,
stumped, stopped, impressed
by the guvnor. There is movement,
subtle, wordless embarrassment.

His fearlessness plunges him forward,
lion brave before men twice his age.
Ankle deep in concrete and more on
the way, out of depth and wide eyed,
shovel push, shovel push, slosh and slap.
'What do I do now, Mr. Old?'

Trystings

I met him after and argument with a wheelbarrow,
Jim said.
We shook hands , eyes saying the same,
showing disinterested interest.
Griff and he took the piss out me,
relentlessly,
and yet, I still grew to love him,
learning how to mimic his worldly ways,
and wishing he would like me.
Walking a gravelled, stony track,
both silent,
I to home and a long walk to Berden,
he, to bakers for a pastry,
before hiking his way home to Braughing.
I looked forward to seeing his gruff,
kingly frame again.
I sought his advice, the first time
ever,
'go over his head', he said. 'Go straight
to the top. Accept no less!'. Unknown
to us both, he repeatedly encouraged
me to accept no less, than the
voice from on high.
I seek his counsel yet, for over these
thirty years, and have done over as many
lifetimes, I'm sure.
His grizzled chops Merlins me still.
I only know this,
that he with furrowed brow
and Souls on his mind,
that if ever I was the thousandth man,
then, as I standing in his light,
he must be, the nine hundred
and ninety ninth.

And I'm Called

A scorpion surrounded by
a ring of fire,
sees death close in from
all around,
and its body on a night,
sand pyre.

Frozen by fear, its tail taut,
raised in the air.
The deathly sting, black,
shiny and glistening,
it wishes it was not there, then.

With a downward thrust in
a perfect aim,
a split second is all the curled tail
needs, snapping down,
when I hear it scream in its dying breath,
hissing, calling my name.

Monet's Morning Again

November gold shimmering, blinding;
Nature is on fire, scintillating.
Trees muted in peach, pink,
Terracotta, lime yellow and bottle green.

Layered, stepped tips soft, stacked arrowheads,
Fluffy in the morning damp sunsplash.
Green hillocks dotted white sheeepishly,
Glisten as crystal, and bulky brown trunks

Carry it all effortlessly, Herculean.
Clawed roots hold the landscape jealously,

Shaled peaks defy everything and bask
Under pale blue and grey strokes, pastel

Gentle, November sharp and inescapable.
These Shropshire hills flashing by,
Of earthy brown autumn fragrance
Give pleasant scents, and a pleasant sense

To this new fresh freedom.
In joy of beauty, pain is released,
Washed and wrung out through struggle.
All replaced and thought of in different colours.

Chimera

I thought I saw you,
standing outside of the
kitchen window.
Staring like a blind man,
I strained my eyes to
focus on your long hair.
I almost moved,
to greet through steam
soaked pane
and realized at once,
that as from the beginning,
you were never there.

Ambushed Joy

When I woke up that morning, I could just tell, taste even that something big was going to happen. I didn't know what, but from some inner reasoning I just knew.

As I rose slowly from the bed, shading my eyes from the sun streaming its way in through the narrow triangular gap in the curtains, my attention was drawn to the vertical row of postcards on the wall above my brother's bed. Like the one's above my own bed, they were from our father. Some showed Arabs in native dress, others showed camels standing before all sorts of Arabian buildings, whilst others showed desert scenes with nomadic black tents, scattered around pools of water and palm trees. All very unusual to my young western eyes.

My brother stirred, grunted and buried his head under his blankets. Just as he was settling into an extra stolen snooze, our mother whisked into our sanctuary in her usual annoying chirpy morning mood. 'C'mon boys, your porridge will be getting cold. Get yerself's washed and doon to the scullery table, quickly now!' Well, whether it was going to be a memorable day or not, there was no getting past the front door without wading through the interminable daily bowl of porridge.

'You can have mine if you want', my brother said as we crammed together at the bathroom sink.

'Have your what?' I said, dozily. I should have known what was coming.

'My porridge. Mum knows I'm never hungry in the mornings, but she always tries to make me eat my porridge'.

'I thought that when we left Scotland we had finished with porridge', I said. Frank rubbed his face dry with a towel like sandpaper; and mumbled in a disgusted muffled voice, 'huh. No such luck!'

At the breakfast table, Frank list-fully stirred his cold tea with his finger. Mum was busy upstairs with our two baby sisters, we could here her West Scotland accent from the kitchen, as she play acted cross at the mess they'd made with their early rising. At the time I was nine, Frank was eight. We had a younger brother Lindsay who was about four or five, and was busy playing happily alone in the corner with some cars. Lindsay was caught in the unhappy situation of being too young for and Frank and I to play with, and too old to play with our sisters. Jeannie and Jan were nappied walking babies really, Jeannie a year or so old and Jan barely ten months. Jan had arrived while dad had been posted abroad.

As I belched heartily from having downed two bowls of porridge, Frank looked up from his now stagnant tea. His normal carefree expression had disappeared. He looked worried.

'When do you think dad'll come home Bert?' He tilted his head to one side, his blue grey eyes piercing an answer from me. I didn't know what to say. Dad, I thought, remembering his broad smiling mustached face. To my fleeting shame I couldn't remember the last time I had thought of dad. It hurt too much. I felt a lump growing in my throat and my eyes begin to water. God in heaven how we missed him.

'I don't know', I said quietly. 'It can't be long now, he went away last summer and it's summer again, now'.

'I hate the army', Frank said. 'I hate it, dad's always away, he's never home'.

He stood up and went and leaned against the sink, staring morosely out of the window into the wild unkempt garden. In a flash of anger, Frank blurted out,

'I bet he wont come home. Some stinking Arab'll get him! I'll kill all the Arabs when I grow up if he doesn't come home!' I'd never seen him looking so sad before, I wanted to do or say something. Instead I looked hopelessly on, paralysed by conscience as if it was my fault. For once big brother didn't have any smart answers, no soothing words with which to caress with.

At that moment, mum came into the kitchen with a baby sister tucked under each arm. 'Right boys, stop ya ditherin' an' get yourselves off to school. Your satchels are by the front door, now off ye go and don't be late coming hame from school tonight. Make sure ye come hame together'.

'why mum?, I asked rising to make way for the girl's morning ritual, as they were deftly and gently laid on their backs on the table top. Lifting her face with a slight grimace from a pair of pungent nappies, mum turned to us both with with a mysterious smile.

'Your uncle David's coming with a present tonight, that's why'. Frank sprang back into life with an expectant smile on his face.

'Is he bringing another telly mum, a bigger one like he said, off the back of...',

'No son', mum interrupted quickly. 'It's something much better than that. Now, away with the pair of you, or you'll be late'. I couldn't help notice a tinge of tenderness creeping into mum's sometimes stern speech. It was a tone I recognized though, although at that moment I never made any connections. Frank and I had heard it lots of times whenever we caught mum crying over dad's photo in uniform. At times like that, all we could do was tell her that we loved her and missed dad too, which usually made her cry all the more.

We each kissed her hurriedly and emerged into the Windsor sunshine, and dressed in our usual his and his blue shorts and shirt, we ambled into a small crowd of other army kids making their way to school. By the time we had reached the end of the street, Frank had disappeared. Then of a sudden I was joined by my friend Allen, a shorter and rounder boy than I. He came quickly out of the crowd, swamped in an ill fitting grey flannel shorts and a baggy red woolly jumper, despite the morning sun. His spiky ginger hair protruded over the top like a beacon, reflecting startlingly as it did the sun's rays.

'What's up then, Allen? You look a bit cheesed off'. Allen shuffled restlessly beside me for a few seconds, dragging his feet and in a reluctant tone, said,

'oh, I'm just tired. I was up late last night watching the telly with the babysitter. Mum was out, as usual', and he yawned and fell silent again. A few yards further on, he said, 'actually Robert, I had a terrible nightmare last night about my dad. And every time I woke up scared and tried to go back to sleep, I just kept having the same dream again. It was really aweful!' He sighed deeply, then said, 'I just wish he would come home'. I sighed too, 'I know what you mean'.

Our little troop had by now thinned out as we neared the school grounds. Our faces blended in with all the other non-army brats, none of us any different to look at, we could have been absorbed into any crowd of any school kids in any town anywhere. The only thing that separated us from the civvy kids was the fact that our fathers were thousands of miles away somewhere in Aden, fighting Arabs.

'What happened then?' When Allen didn't answer, I turned to look at him and saw that he was miles away, deep in thought. 'What happened where, what are you on about?' Allen looked at me as if I'd come from another planet, or something.

'Your dream, what kept happening in your dream?'

'It wasn't a dream Robert, it was a nightmare!'

'Sorry', I mumbled.

'My dad was trapped in a car and he couldn't get out. It was one of those green army cars, you know!'. I nodded

'There was fire all around the car, I mean it was just completely surrounded by flames. And every time my dad tried to get out, the flames kept getting bigger and bigger, so that even if he could have got out, he couldn't have escaped. It was horrible'. For an uncomfortable moment I thought he was going to start crying.

'Don't worry, he'll be allright. He's a Guardsman remember, no one can beat the Guards. They're the best!' I was convincing myself as well as Allen who was quiet after that.

When we got to the school doors, Allen stopped before going in and looked up at me with his usual cheeky grin. His face totally transformed. 'I've got to be home early tonight, mum said. No dilly dallying, she said. I've to be home to see what the postman's bringing. I don't know what it is, but I hope it's that new bike I've been asking for. Funny....mum seemed more distant than usual'. For only a fleeting second or so, Allen had looked serious, but his impish grin returned just as quickly. 'Just think Bert, I'll be able to cycle to school then'. The school bell rang and in a flash Allen turned and darted down the corridor, his sandals slapping the corridor on the lino like the clapping of eager hands. 'See you later', he shouted back to me.

I hadn't seen much of Frank all that day, we were in different classes, we also had different mates, therefore rarely mixing during break times. My last class of the day was English, and we were all taking turns reciting passages from C.S. Lewis', 'The Lion, The Witch and The Wardrobe'. I was completely absorbed in the story, so much so that when Mrs. Sizer, our teacher, made an unexpected announcement, I resented the intrusion into my reverie.

'Will all the children who have fathers serving in Aden, please leave the classroom quietly and make their way straight home. And Bert',

'yes, Mrs. Sizer',

'please be sure to to meet Frank and go home together, will you. See you all tomorrow. Mandy?

'Yes Mrs. Sizer',

'carry on from paragraph four, please'.

The few of us with soldier dads duly left the class, and whilst glad to be getting away early we were equally mystified as to what was going on. I found Frank waiting impatiently outside the school gate. His expression said, 'what's going on?' Though he said nothing. As we left for home, I caught a glimpse of Allen's red jumper and fiery hair dashing round the corner. Excitement was ringing in the air, and unconsciously, our paces quickened and we found ourselves rushing home with the other army brats. We turned the corner of our street, and our hearts leapt into our mouths. On some of the doorsteps there were soldiers in fatigues hugging wives and children, there was a lot of joyful tear-filled reunion. 'Come on!', Frank shouted. 'They're back, dad's home!'. It was too good to be true. We raced down our tree lined street, careered over the polished cardinal red doorstep, through the partially opened door and straight into the huge arms of our great big Welsh Guardsman dad.

'Hello boys, dad's home now'. With smiling tear stained eyes, he picked us both up in each arm and swung us round and round 'til we were almost giddy. Mum came out of the kitchen behind him looking absolutely radiant, tears streaming down onto her immaculate white blouse. Grant and I began bubbling with joy like a couple of babies. Dad was home! In the swirl of excitement and laughter, I remember seeing Frank picking up little Lindsay, crying, 'he's homes Linds', dad's home!' There was a joy in our little brother's eyes, that on its own nearly moved me to further tears. Smiling from ear to ear, Lindsay still had two Corgi cars in each hand, he would never let go of his beloved cars.

Dad went over to his long green army kit bag, from it he pulled out two equally long, slim green cases. 'Yer we are boys, see what I've got for you now. Mam's said you've been good boys while I was away. Look yur now, see what dad's got for you my lovely boys'. What a joy just to hear that deep resonating Welsh accent again. In haste, Frank and I hurriedly emptied the cases and to our amazement saw two of the best fishing rods we'd ever clapped eyes on. We were speechless in heaven. 'Well boys, do you like them, then?' Like them, we loved them. Aside from his homecoming, they were the best present we'd ever had. And the old smells, his Old Spice after shave, the raw manly sweat through his camouflage jacket, we didn't even mind when he rubbed our cheeks red raw in teasing fun with his unshaved chin. Mum, stole cuddles between us, and Frank and I fired a dozen questions at dad. 'Did you shoot many Arabs, dad?'

'Oh, hundreds', he joked.

'Did you use that great big Bren Gun, dad?'

'Aye, all the time boys. Too often for my liking, weighs a ton it does'. Dad sat down finally, on the vinyl green army issue sofa. He swamped it. His broad smiled leapt out from the camouflage kit he was wearing, his eyes shone love on us all. He gathered Frank and me closer to him, we dropped our rods. 'Now, boys. Mam's said you are both doing good at school, so let me see what you've both been doing lately'.

Lovingly encouraged, we dashed to our satchels and pulled out sheets of paper to show him some of our work.

'That's lovely pictures, Frank boy! What birds are they, then?' Frank pointed to each one, 'that's a Kestrel dad. I want one when I get older'.

'And what's that one, then son?'

'That's a red kite dad, I drawed and coloured them myself',

'And I suppose you want one of them too, when you get older, is it?'

'Can I dad, can I?'

'We'll see, we'll see. And what's that your holding, Bert boy. Been writing, 'ave you, son?'

'I'm learning French, dad. This is a drawing of my home and my family, but all the writing's French'. Dad looked at the crayon inscribed Maison. He saw a man in a red tunic and bearskin of the Guards, a short wiry woman in a Lindsay tartan kilt, two young boys, a boy toddler and two bairns in nappies, a nondescript terraced house, and all labeled in an almost tidy joined-up French.

'Aye, I don't need to be able to read French to know that's your family, and you've drawn us all together again, lovely. Tell you what we'll do boys, we'll go to town in the morning and we'll get these lovely pictures put in a frame, is it?' We both jumped with joy at the idea, but our joy was really that dad liked our work, he approved. I think I had a small realization, in that, I had drawn dad in the picture when he was away in Aden. Perhaps inside me, I always knew somehow that he would come home.

In the ebullient chaos that was our army home, Frank and I set up and assembled our rods for the first time. Mum and dad were so engrossed in themselves, that they didn't notice that we nearly knocked several pieces of her porcelain figures, to pieces. Ordinarily, that would almost have been a hanging offence in mum's house-proud world. It would rate about the same criminality as dad flicking his fag ash into a newly cleaned ashtray, and shrugging baffled shoulders in exasperation at mum's protest.

Mum overheard me and Frank telling each other that we were going out to our individual friends' houses, to show them our rods. 'As long as your back in fur yur tea at five, boys. Allright?'

'Yes, mum', we said in unison.

The two rods were the first out the door and into a fading but still warm, sun. Frank nipped off down the street to his mate's and I ran across the road, over to Andrew's house. Rushing along the path, I came to the polished red doorstep, panting. My new amber rod glistened and sparkled as the sun caught the brass connectors and line hoops. I was fit to burst with joy, and I wanted to share it.

I had just about managed to catch my breath, as Andrew's mum came to the door. She looked very tired and unhappy, but I didn't really notice, I was so chuffed.

'Is Andrew coming out to play, Mrs. Woods? I've got a new rod, I want to show him!' My words came out in a rushed torrent of joyous expectation. What she said, blew all that away, instantly. Mrs. Woods look at me from unwavering, distant sad eyes.

'Unfortunately, Andrew wont be coming out to play for a while, Robert'. I didn't understand.

'Andrew's daddy didn't come home today, Robert. He wont be coming home at all, in fact. Never again. There was an ambush, and...'. Her words trailed away as the door slowly closed.

Very shocked, I turned and walked slowly homeward. My head was bowed, and as I looked down at the new rod hanging from my hand, it had lost its sparkle. It looked quite dull and lifeless now.

In God's Name

God: What are you doing there, my Son?

Young Soul: Building a home by the river, Father.

God perplexed: But why my Son, your home is here?

Young Soul: I know Father, but I want to teach the people of your ways, your law and your love.

God Concerned: But they have that. They have the bible.

Young Soul: But they don't know how to read it Father. Once a week they mouth the words and then forget them as soon as they walk into the pub.

God strict: But I need you here my Son. The people with my aid when they seek it, must make their own way.

Young Soul: But Father, if I stay with you too long, you will only send me back here after a time, to do what I'm doing now.

God soothing: My dear Son, you are not qualified to teach my ways.

Young Soul: Father, with respect, I never will be if I stay in heaven. That's also why I need to be here, to learn and teach, and I can still be with you every day. On the mountain top it is easy to be a holy man.

God smiling: My Son, you have already learnt the first lesson.

Winter Respite

Now autumn gold has changed
to a winter white blanket,
bringing a stillness that
seems to pacify the violent city.

Thick flakes cascade gently from
the skies, the birds hide in silence.
Tomorrow, the hunt for food
begins in earnest, warm and buried
under January's ermine lace.

A squirrel absails gracefully and swiftly,
almost careless,down a nearby tree looking for
a hidden hoard. As he digs, hopeful sparrows
watch, waiting for a chance to hoik, furtively
a nut or two while bullying starlings crowd them out

impatiently squawking. Fifteen minutes on a
subterranean train, and I ascend into crisp
Virginia air. A bracing walk, a pipe's distance
from the station, and I arrive at a friend's empty house.
I wait, embracing the still garden.

A distant woodpecker rat – tat taps himself warm,
as my motionless body begins to feel the cold.
The sun, somewhere behind me, casts violet,
changing into its nightclothes, crimson
streaking through the trees.

To defeat the cold, I become one with it,
eliminating the thought that it lies outside
of me. I am cold, it is cold,
we are cold together,
and it's warmer than wishing I was warmer.

Entranced with the silent nature, my eyes
catch sight of a red cardinal
swooping from tree to tree, like a guided
gash red plume in the twilight, a deva,
wrapped in a flaming quilt of fire.

The night draws its curtain closer now,
wood smoke billowing from neighbouring chimneys,
wafting windless upward among still, watching trees.
A pair of squirrels now dance together
on the branches of a bare beech.

My oneness with nature deserts me
as my body shivers and shakes.
It is nothing and it matters not,
for today I was close to it and the spell
is only broken for a while.

Too Soon

Is fate kind or cruel?
So late to make us meet,
too soon to make us part.
And yet, seeming cruel is kind
to set the chance at all.
Fiery friendship all a'spark,
elusive when sought,
potent with imagery, arriving
arriving unexpected, like a railroader
on a solitary track.
Then hearts, firing like
spark plugs, combustion storms
the veins. Darting flashes outshine
from your blue eyes, and
magnetic attraction reigns.
Cruel or kind, this fate thing?
It wears an actor's mask,
frowning one minute, turns
and reveals a smile the next.
Will time and distance stop
the waves? No more than beaches
stop the sea. Intercontinental
thinking, thought waves to and fro,
a heartfelt presence and
warmth a'glow in mind, will
see two foreign travelers,
a Scandinavian and a Celt,
smiling at the memory of
the cruelly short-lived
meeting, that the harsh hand
of fate to them had kindly dealt.

Slumbering Coals

I have never seen Hekla,
but I have met her reflection.

Her lava has never burnt me,
though I have felt her heat,
blazing fiery red,
in strokes of painted oils.

Her mellow heart has touched me,
from moody, pastel blue canvasses,
like her compassion for her people.

Her slumbering embers,
conflicting with her intensity,
have I known, in one who calls me brother.

Hekla, Helga, it's all the same to me.

After the Beach

Sunshine rising open windowed,
dancing off our eyes.
The warmth of intimacy
passes between us,
passes, and becomes
a twnkling memory.

Pain looms ahead
in alienation and
a switching of affection.
Thought resisting lip
biting battles, a wash of
emptiness and ugly jealousy.

In the pain I wonder
the worth of a touch
of denimed thigh,
or your hand clasped
in mine, and I dream;
the night's union,

satisfying a oneness
and my morning
after sensual memory.
Today, tomorrow, I
know I'll miss you,
or forget you.

Hand In Hand

If I should cross the
    barrier,
        and tread where my feet
            should not raise dust,
                forgive me.

                    If I should bend too much,
                    the unspoken rules,
                    placing my voice where
                    ears should not hear,
                    forgive me.

For in life, as in the future
    I'll walk always
        with my heart in yours. With
                my hand clasped in yours as
                it reaches to pull me out,
                of the hole;
                mine envelopes
                yours,
                to free you also.

Out of Synch

He's sitting on my shoulder,
I pretend I can't see him,
knowing he knows I know.

While I grow tired
of human frailties
and inhumanity,

I try to exercise compassion,
realising, I'll only
become angry gain.

And he still waits, patiently
drumming his fingers,
until I face the inevitable,

finally accepting his way
as my only way, kidding myself
it's not the way to go.

In the bubbles, I hold my breath,
trying to prevent drowning
while drowning in blindness.

Bradman Bash Taqi

You gave me insight into your people,
your culture your roots, your land.
You shared with me the voice of a
thousand struggles against my race
and their self righteous ignorance.
And this white man's eyes are wider
and wiser for the experience.

In your fiery pride, your eyes light
up with the blaze of a thousand
tribesmen, and I see all your forefathers
defiance, determination and destruction
at the hands of the red-coated riflemen.
And this white man's eyes are wider
and wiser for the experience.

The futile spear against cannon and
bomb, a scarlet scourge and royal
domination, a ruling blow on your
royal abomination, the images pierce
my mind and imagination.
And yes, this white man's eyes are
wider and wiser for the experience.

Moving On

Stand. The river bristles,
weaves its way around stones,
rose bay willow and the hundred
grains that make up a silty existence.

Stand. The river roars,
bringing with it the wreckage
from upper fields, bringing water,
life and yet a death.

Stand. Stand still,
the river brings peace now,
the flotsam of sorrow
diluted into rivulets

of quietness. The rippling
rushing water, cleansing,

refreshing, exhilarating cold.
I will live like the river,

never divorced from
my source, yet moving,
moving on. Coming back
through valleys and peaks,

sometimes quiet and gentle,
in ripples, and sometimes
roaring over boulders and rocks,
finding, making my way,

seeping through everything,
like one great body of water.

The Stranger In The Park

It was a fine spring morning when I met him. I had left our flat in a state of sadness and borderline depression, having had an ugly row with my lovely lady. I had then decided that I needed peace and sanctuary. 'An Opera Singer and a Mason, I told you it would never work'. It wasn't the first time I had heard this thrown at me almost accusingly; it never ceased to amaze me that the woman had conveniently forgotten to remember that it was she that had sought me out. 'If you will insist on thinking so, then it will be so', was my answer as I left the house in frustration. However, while on my way to a temporary job I visited a beer and liquor shop and bought some cans and a pint of Jaegermeister, herb liquor. The intention being to drown my sorrows and contemplate my future in the relative peace and calm of one of the many small parks in the town of Plauen.

As I approached the park after and uphill walk of a mile or so over uneven cobbled streets, I wondered at the beauty of the budding Chestnut trees and the symphony of song from the birds that called the park their home. I arrived a little after seven in the morning, sat myself down on one of the wooden slatted benches, red paint peeling and like the rest of the benches, sunken out of level. I was alone with only the birds and the trees for company. I reflected upon the senseless row with my loved one as I pulled a can of beer open with a tchsssh and opened the screw top of the Jaegermeister and drew off a longish slug, followed by another chaser of the fine German beer. I'd had a heavy night on the ale the night before and my nerves were shattered, so this morning I suffered from a mixture of too much ooch and too much verbal violence. I must have been tired, because before I knew it I had dropped off into a deep doze. It seemed that I had slept for ages, but upon awakening and checking my watch, I saw that in fact I had only been asleep for twenty minutes or so. I rubbed my eyes, took refreshment from my liquid horde and realised that an old man had joined my company.

He had in his hand what looked like a bottle of vodka and he intermittently sipped at it. Although I actually wanted to be alone, there was a presence about him that drew me towards him. It would be yet difficult for me to explain exactly what that presence was. After all, an old man wearing a very old, somewhat tattered black trench coat, drinking vodka early in the morning is hardly an attractive image. Hypocritical? Certainly. It's amazing what we will accept in our selves and yet not in another. Nonetheless I greeted him in the German. He merely nodded without looking at me and replied, 'morgen'. I pulled out my tobacco, papers and lighter from my shirt pocket and began rolling a cigarette. As I rolled, I furtively took a closer look at the quiet old man beside me. He was huge. I myself am six foot four minimum, broad shouldered and of good build. Sitting next to this old man I felt small. As you may imagine that is a rare experience for me, and one which in a perverse way I enjoy, simply because it doesn't often happen. His shoulders beneath the trench coat were broader and I imagined more muscular than mine. His legs outstretched before me were longer than mine. I looked at his hands. People have remarked that my hands are like hams, but his were a mixture of massive iron gentleness in finely sculptured proportions. Delicate and yet possessing undeniable great strength. He kept looking straight ahead, calmly pondering whatever it was he was observing. It could have been the huge Chestnut tree standing before us, or the fine Baroque German architecture of the buildings on the street opposite. I too looked in the same direction and saw a mixture of fine plaster mouldings under green, copper balconies. I saw a smiling sun wreathed in what appeared to be flowing flames of fire. Above the window openings, faces of maidens with the Star of David on their foreheads. A legacy of the once strong Jewish community who existed in the town before the war. A sad reminder of all the Jews that were sent to the camps, none returned, not one, like a blister of shame in the minds of the populace.

I nonchalantly stretched my legs out before me, moulding my frame into the form of the bench. I continued to observe the man, while casually smoking my roll up. He appeared to have a countenance of youthful antiquity, lines deeply engraved on his face as if of granite. A clear skin which put my own tattered chops to shame, clean-shaven his nose large but finely proportioned like the rest of his body. There was no sagging skin, no liver spots, and a high forehead light and deep channels running across it like the tributaries of the Nile. I extinguished my cigarette and nipped into the bushes for a pee, returning I noticed his eyes. They were the bluest of blue, steady, clear, bright and intense. As I passed him to return to my seat, his gaze never shifted. It was as though I wasn't there. I noticed also that whilst he was almost hairless, there was a remnant of colour among the grey threads of his hair. I noticed at once that in his early years he must have been a redhead as I myself am.

I returned to my thoughts and pondered my miserable situation. No work, no dole, no social security whatsoever, the stress of which of course added to the disharmony on the home front. I wondered also at the human condition, whereby a person can have the patience of a saint with strangers and acquaintances and yet have so short a fuse in temper with an intimate partner. It seemed so alien to my nature and aspirations.

Sometimes I was just sick of myself and what I'd become. Senseless, meaningless and yet for the conflicts to arise there must have been something there, something within these whirling hurricanes of personality disparages that I had to learn. It was then, as I rolled another cigarette, the old man spoke.

'It's a question of perspectives', he said in German. He hadn't turned his head and for a moment I wasn't sure if he was talking to me, or just verbalizing his own thoughts. I shrugged and looked away from him, seeking solace in the fresh shoots of green of the Chestnuts and Silver Birches. From the corner of my eye I saw the flash of his bottle rise, stop momentarily and lowered again. 'Perspectives', he repeated. The bottle flashed quickly up and down again. I turned and saw that his gaze hadn't moved from its location. I rubbed my cigarette out with my boot, and asked, 'what do you mean   exactly?' I stared at him with my elbows haunched upon my knees. I wanted another drink, but for the moment I was happy and intrigued to turn my thoughts in another direction. After a few moments silence, I relented and reached for the can and the bottle, and drank from each of them. 'Do you live at the bottom of the hill, the middle of it or at the top?', he asked. He still hadn't turned his head to look at me; I started to wonder if the vodka he was drinking had began playing tricks with his own perspectives.

'Are you asking me?'

'Do you see anyone else in the park?' I actually looked around. No. There was nobody else, just the circling traffic around the square, which gave the park a sense of detachment. I thought for a moment. 'What hill?' At first I imagined he meant the hill I'd just climbed to reach the park.

'The hill where you live', he said quietly. I thought again, I didn't live on a hill. I lived in an old turreted apartment at the bottom of the valley, next to a stream. No, no hills, except for the ones that surrounded the valley itself. 'No, I don't live on a hill', I answered. 'Surrounded by them, but not on one'.

'Your life is a hill', he said evenly and took another swig. I took the cue and had a couple of belts myself. 'Excuse me, I may be missing something, but I don't understand what you mean'. Having rolled another cigarette, I inhaled a welcome drag and heard him grunt, disparagingly, 'hmmm'.

'Believe that do you?' I almost choked on the smoke. Who was this man?

'Who are you?', I asked.

'What's that to do with the question?'

'Which question?'

'Where you are on the hill'.

'Oh', I said stupidly. 'That question. We haven't met before, have we?'

'Did you think we met by chance? But you still haven't answered my question, have you?' I thought about it. I was getting lost here somewhere. 'I take it the question is hypothetical, or allegorical. Is it?'

'Is it?' He raised his bottle once more and took such a long swig, that even I, as a confirmed slurper would have had trouble getting it down without choking. I had to think. If I don't live on a hill, then what on earth was he talking about?' I myself took another drink, and felt the uncomfortable sensation of being probed. I wanted to ignore this stranger, this giant exuded the effect of knowing something of me that seemed to me, hidden. I was not comfortable with that idea. After all, it was only an idea. Wasn't it?

At the end of the day, I had come to the park in search of peace and solace, as a prelude to a day's work. Apart from wanting to temporarily wallow in self-pity and misery, I yearned to find a middle ground whereby I could find a middle ground, balance my inner life with that which was happening outside of myself. I was seeking a balance, between necessary materialistic living and my domestic existence, something more enriching. I had to face it, at this moment in time prospects seemed more elusive than possible.

'It's a question of perspectives', he repeated, and still his gaze hadn't shifted. I thought I'd be smart. 'Where are you on the hill then?'

'Oh, I'm sitting on the pinnacle. However, the hill I'm sitting on is a foothill compared to the mountain ranges surrounding us' Us? As far as I knew, I was sitting in a park in the middle of a small city.

'How does the surrounding landscape look like from where you are looking?' Easy. I described the park, the birds, trees, the traffic and the beautiful post-war architecture and the wonderful mythological motifs of fine plastering that could be seen through and beyond the trees.

'So you really believe that you are here in this park, do you?'
'Where else would I be?'

'At the moment, you are sitting on my hill. Its quite dizzying when one's not quite used to it, isn't it?' That was it! Time for another fag! I rolled and lit it and wondered perhaps if I'd had too much of the raw stuff. 'How did you get here this morning?', he asked.

'Why are you so interested? I came here this morning to work and try to settle a personal storm. If you don't mind, I'd rather be left in peace'.

'But that's the whole point'. He spoke soothingly, 'you're not in peace are you? More like in pieces, you've brought your storm with you, haven't you?' I felt anger rising and the sense of something of my being was being violated.

I looked at my pocket watch, observed the time and told the stranger that I was due to work. 'If I don't get started, I won't get finished.' I looked at him intensely wondering who the fuck he was, intruding upon my reason to be. Never mind, I resolved myself. What did it matter, who was I? Just another drunk in the park. Fine by me, just leave me alone. I gathered my liquid rations together, and stood up to go. 'Nice speaking to you'. Why on earth did I say that? It wasn't nice at all. He'd jogged my thinking processes, which wasn't a bad thing in itself. However, the mind was spinning and as private person I felt invaded. Why?

For the first time he turned and looked at me, his eyes were like gentle razor blades, sun reflecting, unthreatening and yet penetrating. 'We'll see each other again', he said in a deep soporific voice. 'Will we?', I asked. He seemed so sure. 'I repeat', he added. 'Do you think everything is pure chance? It's all a matter of perspectives'. With that I left him to his vodka and his musings

I crossed the busy junction and entered the old building. Ascending the dusty stairwell, I arrived into one of the two flats on the top floor. It was a horrid job, entailing scraping all the old wallpaper from the walls. The building having been built in DDR times, was constructed of concrete slabs which were bolted together. The old thick wallpaper, stuck as it was to the concrete, was extremely hard to remove. The patterns were rolled cut outs of flowers and swirls, the colours insipid greys, beige and browns. Lacking any artistic qualities whatsoever, they were grey and foreboding, reflecting the mentality of the state that built them. To me it all said absolutely nothing except, suppression.

The work required gallons of water and a ton of sweat and elbow grease. As an unemployed bricklayer, I had accepted the work purely for survival money. The amount to be earned would in no ways help with my rent arrears; but at least it was something. There were two ways of getting through the despicable task. One was to become sufficiently lashed that I didn't care any more, or to try and remain detached from the job and just get on with it. I opted for a combination of the two. I already felt the effects of the liquor and the beer, but retained control of my mind and my emotions, (or so I thought). Despite the ache in my arms and legs from the previous days work, and running up and down the flights of stairs for water, my body felt up to the task ahead. The only obstacle I could see was the lethargic apathy within myself. I took a couple of slugs from each bottle and deciding there was nothing else for it. I picked up the high pressure garden squirter, the scraper and began.

First pumping the container to gain pressure and then showering the wall with a mixture of water and wallpaper remover. The surface became soaked through and I began to scrape. Scrape, scrape, scrape. Here a bit and here a piece that rolled of the walls by gravity. Sweat forming on my forehead. Scrape, scrape. Sweat beginning to pool under my armpits and my back. In the boundaries of my hearing, the birds are singing, the sky was blue and the sun shone fiercely. Trees began to bloom, so you may ask, what was my problem? Its all a matter of perspectives the old man had said. I began to focus on the job, and slowly I found a rhythm; scrape peel, scrape peel. The grating sounds of my plasterers trowel ringing throughout the empty building, the noise echoing where everywhere was quiet. That barren quietude, only derelict houses have.

Within a few minutes my body started to ache with a vengeance, my arms, wrists and hands, the muscles of my fingers where I gripped the trowel too hard. Relax, relax the muscles and observe damn you! Watch the hands, watch the paper, observe the point where the blade scrapes between the paper and the concrete. Watch! Watch! Let the aches go, don't push too hard, slowly, slowly let the tool and the surface work together, just provide the energy.

Where was all this coming from? Who was telling me this? I fought to do the very things that were coming to mind, and still the aches were there while the sweat dripped from my forehead like a watering can. Then a thought struck me, don't fight it, don't try too hard, gently, step back and observe. I stopped and took a drink, allowing the steam of my exertions to cool down. I rolled and lit a cigarette, standing looking at the wall. I decide upon another tactic, this time I wouldn't charge into it, I would approach using some techniques I'd learned in my craft. Namely, observing the work surfaces between the two points of contact. So come on, I told myself, apply it!

So without pushing too hard and not gripping the trowel too tightly, watching the working surface, I found strangely enough that I was able at first to watch my hands, and then my arms. The motion rhythmic and seeming to move by its own energy, unhurried, without lethargy and it bringing a clarity of mind I hadn't experienced for a long time. In observing the hateful task without hate, I was beginning to find a center point; there was space, light and energy. I found myself to my surprise in the present moment; I wasn't in the sorrow of the morning or in the imagined future. I was there now. Scraping, scraping, peeling, peeling, scrape, scrape, peel, peel, watching, observing. The working surface doing its own work, I merely an instrument, and in a sharp moment I knew timelessness. I stopped and wondered at the phenomena I was experiencing; it was then I heard his voice again. 'Its all a matter of perspectives'. Then my mind, that wicked slayer of the real started to play games, seeking robber baron majesty over my new found dominion. The monkey in the head tried to dance with me and entice me with trappings of elation and sorrow; a combination doomed to failure and sure to bring suffering. Had I learnt so much in so few minutes? Was I really beginning to get a grasp of the idea of perspectives? Or was I just remembering lessons taught to me as an aspirant philosopher. I don't know. All I was sure of, was that I wanted to guard this conquest so bitterly wrought from sorrow, confusion and bitter loneliness.

In my newly attained equilibrium I tried again. Scrape, push, sweat, scrape push, sweat. Suddenly from nowhere, from out of the dark, I was inundated with flooding thoughts of joy; elated false joy of going home and telling my lady that everything would be all right. Wanting to share the joy of what I had re-discovered, but realised that as soon as I walked in the door smelling of booze, the whole viscous circle of patterns would start whirring again. Wishing in my heart that it would not be so, but knowing full well it would be. Then the opposite pole. Worrying about finances, the desperation, and the tax man and wondering why on earth I was still here in this God forsaken hole of former East Germany. Huh, I thought, I've never been anywhere for much longer than three or four years, and yet after nearly five here I was still. The lady of course was the reason.

The dance in the mind continued, at once oscillating between the thoughts of the long awaited job that would clear the debts, buy the new car and buy me time to finally finish the book I'd been writing for ten years or more. Where was I on my hill? If the stranger in the park meant what I thought he meant, then I was scratching in the dark scary forest of the foothills. Yet just a few moments before, I was able to see things differently, from another perspective.

Then something else happened, I rose out of the woods and found myself sitting maybe half way up the foothills, contemplating events below me. I watched the thoughts closely as they clamoured for my attention, but I was not going to give into them. I found that as I gave less and less attention to them and focused on the job in hand, that I was able to gain more control over what I wanted to think. In the space between the little vipers, I was able to let the thoughts come and go, I was able to place my mind in that space between thoughts.

At first for only a fraction of a second, but slowly but surely the space in between lengthened and I could maintain a sense of timelessness and space. I was neither elated nor depressed, no longer controlled by unwanted worries or megalomaniac joy. I just was, just in the present again. By this time I had practically finished the first room, sloppy, sticky paper up to my ankles, so decided to take a break.

I stepped out on to the balcony at the rear of the house and into the blazing sun. The safety bars had been removed and I suddenly felt exposed. I gingerly looked over the edge, it was quite a way down and as the flutters in my stomach increased, I stepped back inside to safety and sat myself down, cross-legged and Hindu style. I could see the tops of the trees clearly; the exposed trunks and roots that crept from the trunks like gnarled fingers. Beyond, all the hoses and gardens that formed a square. The sun bathed my face and I felt the heat at once drying existing sweat and yet creating more, the alcohol. I lit a roll up and inhaled deeply the rich, strong tobacco. As there was little breeze, I absently blew smoke rings and watched as they passed from the balcony into the air, to be dissipated and carried away to nothingness, like thoughts. Then an idea occurred to me. I from the balcony, could see what was going on below, who was coming round the corner, (which from below I would be unable to), was this then not dissimilar to the experience I'd just had when I was able to watch my body and my mind detachedly working? Checking nobody was below, I flicked my cigarette over edge and watched it crash like a smoking plane and tried an experiment.

As a youth I had been involved in various spiritual and esoteric groups. Each one had something different to offer and each approached the subject of the nature of life from a different angle. But the one thing they all had in common and the one thing they all came back to, was the Sacred mantra OM. If the OM is at the top of the tree of all mantras, then the main branch supporting that tree is the mantra, OM MANI PADME HUM, which means the jewel in the lotus. So with the mantra in mind and remembering to observe the 'working surface', I approached the task differently.

I stood still for a few moments listening to my breath, the birds singing outside and to the nearest and furthest sounds. Concurrently, I looked at my body as an extension of my Self and not the consummation of it. I picked up the broom and swept the debris into a centre pile ready for bagging. As I watched the broom sweep across the floor, I repeated inwardly to myself, OM MANI PADME HUM, OM MANI PADME HUM. At first, the same thing happened as when I tried to watch the working surfaces alone, the thoughts began to clammer for my attention, so instead I voiced the mantra that I might hear it above the circling thoughts. Of course I wasn't able to completely stop the thoughts; I don't think it's important to do so. However, I was able to slow the thinking process down so that once again I could detach from the mental noise, and exert control over what I wanted to think and give attention to. That was the difference.

I then turned the mantra inward and tried to focus it in the central point in my forehead, and again the same thing started to happen. It was as if the thoughts had seen an opportunity of breaking through my concentration, and had decided to rush me in an attempt to regain possession. This time I was ready for them, armed and ready; my ex-soldier father would have been proud of me had it been another battlefield.

As the rush approached I sped up the mantra in my mind without losing my concentration on it, nor did I forget to observe my hands working in unison with the broom and the surface of the floor. In a short while I was able to sustain longer periods of focus between the onslaught of circling thoughts and inner conversations. In truth, I began to see that I was having inner conversations consciously, which had formerly been unconscious. What a remarkable discovery!

Not only was I able to exert a measure of control over my physical activities, I also found that the same principle of observing the work surface applied to the activities of the mind. I stopped in my track.

I was called to remember an incident in my youth. I was nearing my eighteenth birthday, and at that time I attended a school of philosophy in London a couple of nights a week. I had loved the place and all it taught. It laid an accentuation on the Vedas, the ancient Hindu teachings, Ouspensky, Gurdjieff and Marsilio Ficino. In a class one evening our teacher asked the question where we had observed the workings of observing 'working surfaces'. As a trainee bricklayer, it was in that field that I practised the combined philosophies. For as an example I talked of the laying of the mortar from the trowel onto the bricks, then the evening out of the mortar surface and the laying of the brick onto the bed. Then buttering another vertical joint onto a brick and repeating the process, all the while cleaning the excess mortar off the bricks with the trowel and maintaining focus and attention to all the actions and different working surfaces. Between each surface, and this is the point.

As I spoke; which I rarely did, I felt embarrassed before the class, mainly because they were all older than myself and were comprised of accountants, bankers, lawyers, and publishers, etc: One very well dressed and well to do man asked, 'but what use is that in every day living?' The teacher, a British born Asian looked at me knowingly. I was extremely embarrassed as I said, 'because the same principle applies to the working surface of the mind'. The teacher's response was heart warming. 'Our young friend is correct, ladies and gentlemen. The same principle does apply to the working surfaces of the mind'. Unfortunately, it was this prevalent attitude of what can an apprentice bricklayer possibly know about these things, that determined me to leave the school. Until this day I had forgotten the incident and the lovely language of the Ancient Wisdom, that I had learnt all those years ago.

It was evident to me now standing in this concrete heap, literally scratching a living that the application of these principles; the observation, the focusing beyond the vision of thoughts and using a mantra, that memory was also stirred. Another thought occurred to me. These bare bones of a building had once housed families from all over the eastern block. These rooms had stood witness to all the joys, sorrows and gamut of emotions and thoughts, and I wondered if the building itself carried the energy and memories of all that previous life. Mad? Possibly. Possible? Why not? How far could we stir the memory of what has passed before, and if we could, how? I finished my drinks, put the empties into a sack and decided to ponder those ideas at a later date.

I sat down on the top of the stairs and composed myself in silence. I wanted one more try at finding space within the mind. As I sat, I felt the weight of my seat on the step, the weight beneath my feet and the play of air against my skin. I repeated the exercise of listening outwards to the furthest and gentlest of sounds and began to observe my body, not me as such, rather the vehicle wherein I was housed. This had the effect of allowing me to detach a little from my corporeal tenement, bring me closer to the workings of the mind, once again. Something curios happened. I noticed that as the traffic passed on the busy roads outside, my attention wanted to latch onto the noise of the passing motors, so that when I tried to focus on a still point within, my attention got carried away with different vehicles and then away with thoughts. I tried then not to allow the outside disturbances distract me, which I discovered was not the same thing as listening to all the sounds as a whole. Rather, to let the sounds be where they were or pass where they passed. I then found I could return to that space within the mind and the central stillness in life and continue the exercise. Though of course the lower part of my mind always wanted to grab onto all the distracting noises and lead them onto thoughts.

Perhaps the most important thing that I had rediscovered, was that one can find stillness within the mind, and from that point of stillness all things are possible. Perhaps that is what the poet Milton meant when he said, 'the mind is its own place, and can make a heaven of hell or a hell of heaven'. There it was, not an answer but a key, a small key for a very large lock. It was indeed a matter of perspectives. Not that answers lay in these exercises, rather that the exercises gave me an opportunity to see what was going on more clearly, what was relevant and what was not. Not to be bogged down so much in the grey dark nor so elated as to be totally out of touch. God! Where had I been all this time? Chasing glittering prizes of finance, security and all the things we are taught we must do to be normal. I had been asleep, asleep in dreams and ambitions and the unachievable imagined future. What had I been hiding from? Myself of course.

After I had finished the second room and made everything clean and tidy I swept all the mess into bags and called it a day. During the progress of the work I had applied the two principles, observation and attention and joyful that I had remembered something practical from so long ago, and amazed at myself for having forgotten them. In between times, when I felt the world within the mind was getting the better of me, I would sit or stand and remember. I would stop, look at my hands and run my mind and myself through the process of re-focusing and remembering, until I had re-connected to that point of stillness.

I decided that I had had enough for one day and thought once more of the strange man in the park. I descended the stairwell a little weary but not tired, and certainly not as tired as I had been on previous days. One thing was clear; the exercises were energizing, calling to mind another voice from the past. 'There is always sufficient energy for work done in the present'. I walked back into the park, there was no sign of the old man, only an elderly lady dressed in typically uncloured, practical clothing reminiscent of the days of The Wall, walking her dog lifelessly around the park. I took out my pocket watch and noted the time was a little before five.

My lady friend would already be at the theatre getting ready for her lead role in the evening performance. I wondered what I should do next. The effects of the alcohol had faded and with their departure, came a clarity. The colours of nature were brighter and fuller, and even though the dull, drab grey brownness of the old eastern block surrounded me, still I found a quality of life regained within those neglected walls.

I hadn't heard him approach, but there he was all of a sudden standing in front of me, still wearing his long black trench coat and bearing the same bottle hanging wistfully in his hand. Sitting himself down on the bench beside me, he offered me a drink from his bottle. I wanted to decline, I actually didn't want the effects of alcohol but accepted out of some sense of false courtesy. When I took a slug, I was surprised to find that it wasn't alcohol at all, but instead some kind of water, though totally unlike any tap or mineral water I knew. Those oh so blue eyes watched me with a twinkle of amusement. He could see the puzzlement in my face, no doubt.

'What is that?'

'Oh, an old recipe that was handed down to me. Good isn't it?'

'Certainly is', I said, suddenly feeling even more calm and tranquil.

'I thought you'd gone', I added.

'So have you got an answer to my question?' Although he was looking straight ahead, I could tell he was listening to every word I was going to say. I wouldn't endow him with super powers, but at this point I could have believed he could hear my thoughts too.

'I think so', I replied. 'And I agree with you, it is a matter of perspectives. In answer to your question, let me put it this way. I no longer feel as if I'm foraging amongst the undergrowth of my mind, more a little up the hill just far enough to see over the trees to the hills beyond. It's a much healthier place to be, much healthier'. Smiling I turned to meet his eyes, but he'd gone. I looked quickly from left to right, in front of me and behind, but there was no sign of him.

I was stunned, this was insanity, this could not be real. A sense of uneasiness tried to creep over me, I resisted, not wishing my sanity to implode. I had to get a grip, it made no sense, and yet I knew I hadn't been hallucinating. If I was, I wasn't going to admit it. I rose from the bench and headed home shaking my head in wonderment, and then involuntarily I laughed out loud so heartily people turned to look at me strangely. No wonder! I composed myself and carried on walking with such a sense of at-one-ness, that none of it really mattered anyway. I had decided that I would go to the theatre that night, and watch my lady love playing her fine performance of *Madame Butterfly*, in quite a different light.

Half way home, still centering and at peace, a familiar voice came into my head, this time the old man's voice was in English. 'When you returned to the park, you looked for me and you thought I'd left. You looked again and I was there. If you ever need me, look for me and I will be there. You know how to find me'.

The Waiting Game

The sun rises over the hills
of the valley beyond.
At my back, the crows awake
with a start.
Surrounded by the sounds
of full nature waking up;
a cacophony of birds singing
through the steamy rising mists,
pierced by their song and the
penetrating, golden rays.
There are no fences here,
only the invisible ones, hidden,
behind circling thoughts
of home and loved ones
and the life that waits
patiently, out there.
A canned, unreal voice suddenly
dominates the peace.
The birds stop talking and listen,
as we all must:
'Jones 461,
Jenkins,
Absolom,
Harker,
Akram,
Owen 362,
Griffiths,
Price,
Mitchell,
Wells 868,
report to control now for check off,
last warning!'
I am reminded of T.V. as a youth,
'I am not a number, I am a free man!'
There are no walls here,

only subtle, firm reminders
that home is one hundred
and seventy six nights away.
Time stands still,
is marked only by meal times, sunrise,
sunset and dreams awakening;
punctuated by tinned commands
and sarcasm;
'hands off cocks and put on socks!'
and no amount of cold water
applied vigourously to sleepy
face will chase that dream away.
No mother's comforting arms,
no female tenderness or viciousness,
only non-existent time.
A crow idly, nonchalantly walks
and passes me, even it has not
even the slightest interest in me.
A pair of magpies seek breakfast,
and I wonder is my mate mating yet.
Here, we are all the disenfranchised,
equally nothing.
Warm sun bathes my face,
soothing, encouraging light.
Beyond the out of bounds signs,
life in another system waits,
as I do.
To exist again,
quietly waiting.

Chrysalis

Seemingly stagnant for months one end,
cuccooned and kept cuckoo warm,
this crusted protecting shelter of mine
hangs hard, still and lifeless to the eyes
and touch.

Unseen, this internal eternal, burns
furnace fierce, the scales from
these walls, until the walls themselves
disintegrate under billowing heat.
The fire,

oh heavens, the fire. Sometimes
dubious, timeless creation creates
itself behind this dangling shell,
that hangs, strung like a puppet,
whose sponsorship

threads unknown. My patron's eyes
I have not seen, mere reflections
of his gaze that stir this grub
to transformation, through through
the razored maze,

and destiny unknown, awaits. But
there, a chink of light, a small
accelerating crack, sears this haven
of hell, built by my own hand.
Small spark

of illumination filters through,
sharply beamed and pin-pointing,
embarrassingly accurate, awakens
me from pregnant sleep. Immensely
bright

I look away, but am forced to
stare as the light, increases
in its intensity. The shell
cracks, the strain unbearable
on my ever shifting structures.

The old me dies hard,
and is hard to shake, though die
it must, as dead leaves fall away,
revealing a flower of unnameable
beauty.

The ever growing light, shakes
and shimmers, and my wraps
merely respond. The piercing
light, stirring new limbs,
unknown

and undiscovered. The reward
of patient, painful, putrefaction,
and tis hanging prison falls,
falls away, and yet, more growing
pains, and something

spreads out from me. The light,
bright pain exacting on my
new found wings, stretching
almost out of the sockets
in reaching,

reaching out, feeling cool clear
air. And naturally I, once bound
by my own bonds, flutter and
splutter and fly. Below me,
an old shell,

lifeless,cold and dead.
No sorrow at its leaving,
not now,
not in new
flight.

Femininity

I reflected on my thoughts
 as the moon reflects the rays of the sun.
  And in those same thoughts,
  I saw your face.

   In your face I found mystery, and found
    the urge to discover and renew
     that other scary road that lies
      before all men,

       the road to femininity, mostly
        hidden, and yet, expressed
         and feared simultaneously.
          The dichotomy of men.,

           In your arms and curves
            I wallow and luxuriate, hopeful,
             fearful and expectant of oblivion.
            Instead I saw a tapestry,

           woven and threaded by time
            with images long forgotten;
             mystical, endearing, caught
            in the youthful naivete of childhood.

         Sealed, before the death of innocence
        and the birth of painful consciousness.

With or Without Me

A inner flame,
  Sans moi.
    Burns like diamonds,
      Sans moi.
        Violet splashed radiance,
          Sans moi.
            Inner jewel, find me,
              let that inner flame burn,
              Avec moi.

So Rich It Hurts

Go your own way to your own destruction,
leave me with the slaughtered cows.
I'll bleed inside and out, for love,
sometimes shaking my head in despair.
But when I sleep at nights, I'll see beauty.
I'll foster goodness in honest, empty pockets
and trade shelter for a good day's work.

Love is not a commodity,
it seeks no competitive exchange,
only empty spaces to live in,
and dirty streets to clean,
restoring the blue and green of the planet,
with waves of growth, not greed.
So, I'll walk in the deepest waters,

I'll sing wit the diminishing whales,
bounce with goats on the mountains,
grow with the flowers on the hills.
I'll drink acid rain till it kills me,
and dance with disappearing trees,
and find richness in the wonder of it all.

Valentine Moon

Dance with me beside
the sea break,

under a full moon, when the sea
calm as a lake,
reflects the light of the moon
and our eyes and back.

sing to me of silent sea-shores,
seaweed and gulls,
talk to me of nonsense, poetry
and social mills.

But most of all, dance with me
til our feet are wet,
to the silent celtic harps,

dance with me,
let me spin you around
and fall with you in heaps.

Evening Twist

Oedipus came to call
last night,
I told him to go away
instead,
no, he said, I can't
do that,
so I told him, but mother's
dead,
he stood there smiling,
tipping his hat,
I am your mother, he said.

Thor's Girl

Daughter of the northern lights,
you shared your light with me,
spreading it over my heart
and touching my love, where
my soul knew it not.

Just as the hidden valleys
of your home land, caught
your rays and warmth,
then gone, like the sun behind
a cloud, unseen, still there

and sorely missed. Thor's child,
not of my flesh, yet,
you beat my heart with your
hammer, it thumps and
pounds still.

Visitors

That gentle breeze
   that from the icy north,
      falls upon me as a
         descending stillness.

            Tautness of emotion disappears,
               and bathed they become
                  exalted, and the ideal becomes
                     a manifest reality.

                  I can breath again,
                  I can see again and
                  broad shoulders expand
                  bearing the load.

                  Sometimes fleeting, infinitesimal
                     and at once eternal.
                  I know this light robe, sometimes,
               I've earned the wearing.

            Other times, I dare not
            touch the hem.

Silent Workings

She chooses to walk
with kings, gracing
the company there.

As deft as the ink
flowing from her pen,
that violet smile

once bestowed, gives
light to the eyes
that yet need to

learn to see. Ask,
and her wand will
point and create

those forms, poets
and kings dream of.
Crowned heads stand

quiet and acknowledging,
silent, observing
the light. Her inner

majesty embraces
vermilion, as in
cut glass vase

given to one
who has known
that noble form.

That vase filled
with royal purple,
shades of white lilly

and tall monkshood.
Yet, she chooses the
company of kings.

Ticking

Watching the second hand turn around,
  counting existence in moments of time,
    smiling faces of loved ones come to mind.
      The feelings of their love relived,
        and I find myself richer than the Pope could ever be.

        Tender hearts I have loved and crushed,
        that crushed and loved mine in return.
        Unintended crimes of the heart,
        washed away in tears and forgiveness,
        the shattered dreams strewn like bridal flowers.

        I love to remember tender caresses,
        that warmed my body and filed my mind.
        Those long distant calls of well wishing,
        open my hearts to the joys,
        while pains recede in the tides of time.

      I watched again the second hand,
        to realise time hadn't really moved.
      The scenery had changed, that's all.
    For they are all still here within me;
time doesn't move, but the heart beats eternal.

Pendine Sands

Oh, the sea.
Ever ebullient,
Ever waxing ever waning,
The constancy. Forceful
And often gentle, veils its power
To then crash and thrash and stroke
Us lentil amber, and as a sand dune
I welcome the soft strokes,
that caress my shifting sands.
And then I see differently and am seen
As another. And in those shifting sands
My face changes; at once bearded and again
Clean soft and innocent, wishing to be
Pure once more.
And after the climbing, sighing waves
Slide away, having crept and washed
My unseen Self; that intimate Self
only nature's water can sift through,
then, I see you, feel you and come
from nowhere to somewhere, washed,
new and confusion falls away into certainty.

Crucifixion

Behind the doors of
lack of self worth,
the walls begin to crumble.

The hidden valleys of
desperation, create
even deeper ravines

between Soul and self.
Lost, disorientated by what
is done and that wished,

we die daily, like someone
before, nailed and abused
by our own desires.

Reverie's Delight

Softly, the folds of night
            come closer,
and in the reverie of solitude,
the soul speaks volumes
            in the silence.
Raptured, the mind becomes
a saucer of spiritual milk,
            that dowses
fluttering thoughts. Thrilled,
the being ripples with meaning
            as purpose
slowly, reveals its elusive
            ancient face.

Et Ure For Vera

(A watch for Vera)

Huske at tiden
flyve altid,
mærke den,
men tælle den ikke.
Livet er langt nok for alt
og alt for kort,
for, for meget.

Remember, time
always flies.
Note it,
but don't count it.
Life is long enough for everything,
and too short
for too much.

Bagging

The house straddles
the river and road,
earth to the front,
water to the rear.
The roof poised in the air;
where the three meet
magic is performed,
they say.
I'll sweep the paths
around the house,
gathering brown damp leaves,
and paper fragments
of yesterday, signs of the
ever-present past.

Leaves and papers,
the discarding of excess
baggage, bagged and forgotten.
Oh let me clear the paths
of my mind so.

Empty Voices

I heard a voice today, it came
  softly over the phone.
    There was distance, estrangement
      ringing in its confused tones,
        a sense of loneliness that
          hid behind the words.

              I knew the voice, I knew the words;
              the soft articulate expressions, and
              the gentleness, at once small
              and giant,
              and I wondered why I couldn't place
              the face.

              Then, of course I realized,
              the voice was mine, and
              nobody was listening as
              I talked into an empty
              answer-phone.
              Nobody there.

Equilibrium

It's too nice a day
to be unhappy.
Though my world
changes around me,
freedom is an attitude
I've lost and found.

FanØ

Waves ever lap and surround FanØ,
sometimes thrashing the bare buttocked
dunes,
sometimes caressing the raw flesh of sand,
mimicking the temperamental passions
of man and mistress.
This love is inevitable, as too the tides
of man's love.
As magnetic moon pulls and decides
the thrusts of the sea,
there is something within and without,
that dictates the undulating, wavy
love of woman.
Yet see Narcissus and Hermaphrodite
play with themselves in the mirror;
we are all of us mirrors,
and in our love for each other,
we also love our reflections.
And when we despise those visions
before us,
we despise ourselves, projected and
reflected on the cross of love and pain.

The seething gnawing ocean, eats away
the coastline, and those lands around us,

become smaller,
only to return to the mass below
the veiling sea, creating illusions of
separate identities.
Poor fleshy, land creature we,
aspiring to that God like immortality,
in the embraces of sand and sea,
man ad woman, sink, into the great
dark pool,
lost indistinctly in the dark
swirling hordes.
Better that should rise amid furious
demons, dying, clinging desperately,
and surface like the lost beauties
of Atlantis. Our blackest deeds washed
away and sunk in time, and love,
united in purpose,
remaining intact, individual, universal
and one; sand and sea lovingly
understood.
If this is creation, let's begin again.

Green Slate, Black Hands & French Cigarettes

As his wiry frame puffs with effort,
his wife, curses his laziness,
and yet he ferry's buckets of water,
chisels, trowels and French cigarettes.
Sweating, he flashes me a hopeless smile
of resigned acceptance, while I
grapple black handed with green slate.

A pummeled, moulded fire-back
waits coldly for the new fire.
The raped and broken hearth
almost regains its former shape,
as sweat pours from tired pores,
smelling of yesterday's wine while
yet another beer changes hands.

From behind curly waxed moustaches,
that point and demand respect,
another wry, impish smile escapes.
Kneeling down beside me, his
perfectionist's eye inspects the work,
surveying all he commands,
fussing and worrying.

Grudgingly, happy to see it all
build itself again, he tells me tales
of Gypsies, Flamenco, Spain
and France. I struggle to make
up irreplaceable, lost time.
Time lost during the Master's panic,
then, he tells me, take your time.

Frosted Breath

Lovely, unrelenting
  frosted breath,
    oh, how I sought you
      as I sought my death.

        It's a deft stroke
          the draws the dark
            veil of night
              onto day.

Forever Autumn

In the dull pale light of
          dusk,
          red streaks of sun sink
          behind leafless trees.

Among damp brown
          leaves
          cast timely to the ground,
          I pull up my collar

against a cool chill breeze,
          that
          dances through bare fronds
          and branches with grace and ease.

Drilling

Alone on the platform
she works.
The enormous drill
digs deep, very deep,
penetrating the
crust of a million years.

The only woman on site,
the only person
brave enough to stand
against the howling freezing winds
that buffet the rig. Enough,
to make weaker souls shake.

The oil is a lover, but it's
other riches she seeks,
and deep she digs and deep
she seeks, fulfilling inner life
with meaning
in the challenge.

Fearless in the face of
a truth. Her truth,
hidden beneath the
strata of consciousness.
Consciousness too, is hidden
from the eyes of millions,

who could not,
would not face the
isolation of breaking
out from limitation and
choking constriction;
and by dissolving, achieve.

Down, the wreaking
dark depths below,
vibrate, resonating through
the rod that breaks its
heart to give up its black jewel,
made colourless

with inner sight. Luminous
numinosum pervades.
The gushing pulse of
enrichment, the
only fecundity
tolerable.

The remains remain,
with that and those
who fade under
stolen light, wrought
from the core and caught
in speaking colours, scintillating.

Clear As Crystal

When the large round bee landed on his arm, it didn't wake the old man up. He wasn't sleeping, but anyone walking into his study that afternoon would have thought so, had they not noticed the reclining old gentleman in his well worn low armchair, eyes closed with an expression of focused concentration set about his features. The eyes opened gently to reveal a curious light violet colour to the irises, and the fiery light that shone out of them focused on the small creature with a patient curiosity.

He noticed that the bee was agitated, but this caused him no concern, as all his life he'd maintained an affinity with bees. What did interest him was why the bee was so agitated, its antenna were twitching and as it rubbed its head with its forepaws, its abdomen gyrated and jerked from left to right. As he sat and watched the creature, it became clear that something was very wrong. This was a Waggle-dance he'd never seen before The bee stopped twitching suddenly, just long enough to turn and fly away, exiting the way it had come through the open window. The old man watched it buzz through the garden to disappear, as if literally, into an unusual blazing March sunshine.

The old style black telephone rang into life on his desk. By the third ring he had the handset to his ear. 'Akaya', he answered. 'Yes, I work with bee swarms. No, I don't dispose of them, I accommodate them. I'll be there in half an hour'. He left his study and went outside to his car, an old sedate, bottle green Morris Minor Countryman. Into the back he loaded a large, very old wrinkled brown egg shaped soft leather case, a large blue steel toolbox and a pair of hedge clippers and secateurs. The old car burst sharply into life and Akaya cast a quick glance into the rear view mirror. He nodded and smiled to himself when he saw no excessive smoke coming from the exhaust. In the winter months, he had designed and made an exhaust catalyser, and upon fitting it and trying the end result, he was delighted to see that his little idea made material, worked. The fumes had in effect been cleaned, so contributing in small to reducing pollution. 'One day they'll make it standard', he mused.

'Llamedos Rape Seed Oil Company, Clun. Hmm, never heard of them'. The old car sped jauntily through awakening country lanes, burgeoning with seed pods and early buds just waiting to explode into beauty. Before long, he was traversing the A49 and having reached the small town of Craven Arms, turned left a the hotel roundabout, heading first for Aston-On-Clun and then onto Clun proper. In the middle of the village, he hailed an elderly gentleman coming out of the Sun Inn. As the man leaned down to respond, Mr. Akaya could smell a little real ale on the other's breath. 'I'm looking for Llamedos Oil Company, please'.

'Oh yes, the oil company'. The old man shook his head slightly, musing.

'Bit of trouble with bees, they have',

'Yes, that's why I'm looking for them'.

'You're the bees man, are ye? I've 'eard of you''

'I am. Could you tell me how to find them, please?'

'Of course, though I tell you what. You'll need to be careful, angry they are, the bees. Never known 'em so mad'. The old man's wrinkled brown face, spoke of years labouring on the fields. Bent over with an arm resting on his stick, the old man spoke quietly to Mr. Akaya, almost in conspiratorial tones, 'summat to do with that oil they make, I reckon'. A pause for thought, and then, 'Yep, it'll be the oil'. Akaya looked at him evenly for a quiet moment or two, and asked softly, 'and where will I find them?' The old man raised and pointed his stick and explained.

Following the directions given, Mr. Akaya took the old Morris up a tree lined, steep banked road. As the car reached the brow of the steep incline, he noticed a signposted turning to the left, indicating the location of Llamedos Rape Seed Oil Company. This section of road was unpaved and the colour of cigarette ash, it cut through dense wood which covered the hill he'd just come up, and was one of the hills that made the beauty of Clun Valley famous. The shale track opened up into a large clearing that overlooked the valley and fields below. In the now near midday sun, the Rape fields were golden radiant and scintillated in brilliance, reminiscent of a Monet or Van Goch. The intensity of the bright yellow was almost blinding.

Remaining seated in his car, Akaya looked around the scene. He was immediately struck by the huge size of the industrial plant, its modernity in stark contrast with the old ancient folds of the wooded Shropshire hills. On and around the top right hand corner of the building facing him, Mr. Akaya could see from the car that a largish group of what looked like bees, had gathered. By the look of the insects, they were definitely not happy, in fact it wouldn't be an exaggeration to say that they looked absolutely hopping mad. Beneath the bees, three men in white technician's coats, collars and ties stood milling around with two younger men, in blue boiler suits. Amongst the beautiful, peaceful surroundings, they pointed and gesticulated towards the cluster of frenetic bees. They bore alternate expressions of worry and impatience, and one white coat in particular kept checking his wristwatch as if expecting a train.

One of the boiler-clad younger men, turned from the team and stared for a moment or two at Akaya, still seated behind the wheel of the Morris. A wide smile of recognition broke upon the fresh faced youth, and with a decisive step, he turned and walked quickly towards the old man. Humph, I know this boy, thought Akaya. I'm sure I do. He unfolded his tall, sparse frame from the car and waited for the youth's approach. The boy stood in front of the old man at half a head shorter, and with inquisitive smile. 'Is that you, Mr. Akaya? I remember your old car!'

'You have the advantage of me young man. I recall your face, but your name escapes me'. Akaya shook the outstretched hand and smiled. 'It's Andrew, Mr. Akaya. Remember?, I helped you last year with the swans down at

Serpentine Lake'. Akaya made a move towards the building. 'Ah yes, Andrew. Of course'. He recalled the young man's eagerness and willing help with the dying birds. At the time, Akaya had marked him down with his shock of thick red curly hair and guileless emerald green eyes, as a Soul to watch. 'You were of great help to me with the swans, Andrew. I'm not sure I could have managed it without you'. Andrew blushed feintly, chuffed for the recognition. He said quietly, the smiled lost temporarily, 'I still get a sick feeling to my gut Mr. Akaya, when I think of those poor swans'.

'They're allright now, dear boy', Akaya said quietly. 'They're allright now'. They had walked in slow silence for a few yards, when Akaya asked the lad, 'who's the clock-watcher, then Andrew?' Andrew looked up from watching the ground and glanced across to the other men. 'Oh, that's Davis, one of the bosses. He's always fretting about something!' As Andrew said that, the man Davis drew himself away from the other white coats and approached the pair. He was sweating profusely beneath his white hygiene hat and technician's coat, his eyes flitting from side to side, as if unable to decide what to focus on. He glanced at Andrew and Mr. Akaya as if unsure how to proceed.

'Are you Mr. Akaya, the chap come about the bees? It was Andrew who suggested that you might be able to help us out. Are you a beekeeper? '.

'No, but I am my brother's'. Davis cast a quizzical glance at Andrew, and then smiled a little nervously at Akaya.

'Funny, for some reason I expected you to turn up in a van. I haven't seen one of those old Morris's for years. I'm Davis, Financial Director. Pleased to meet you'.

They shook hands briefly and walked to the corner of the industrial unit, its wide gauge corrugated steel walls towering above them. Right on the soffit edge of the roof, there hung a large group of bees clumped together en mass, while many more flew around desperately, angrily, as though in panic. 'There's, the problem, Mr. Akaya. We don't know why they're grouping up there, but we do know that they're flying into the plant and causing havoc amongst the staff, to the point where they can't work properly. Half of the staff are off work suffering multiple stings. And worse still, they're clogging up the machinery and getting into the processing. Look at the ground and the floor inside, dead bees all over the place, hundreds of them'.

'And of course', added Mr. Akaya, 'halted processing equates as halted profits'. There was a hint of sarcasm in Mr. Akaya's tone, but it was lost on the other. Davis looked up at Akaya, the wrinkles on his forehead gone, so pleased was he that help was at hand.

'You're absolutely right, Mr. Akaya. I'm glad you understand!'

'But I am more concerned as to why the bees are behaving so angrily. Do you mind if I borrow Andrew for an hour or so?' Davis looked from Akaya to Andrew and back.

'No, of course not. If Andrew doesn't mind'. The two men looked at Andrew, who smiled and said, 'I'd love to help if I can'.

'Good, then I'll leave you to it, then'. Davis left the two and rejoined his colleagues.

The oil company's buildings formed a square on top of the hill, and Akaya had noticed that the complex was invisible from the villages and roads below. It was clear that it had been designed so as to 'fit in'. Although it was clear to Akaya's mind, that short of covering all the buildings with foliage, the industrial site would always be an ugly scar on the countryside. Beyond the outermost warehouse, the fields were all turned to rape seed oil plants. Akaya and Andrew had walked behind the large warehouse and were looking over the fields, Akaya's eyes intent, searching. 'What are we looking for, Mr. Akaya?'

'We are looking for the main swarm, Andrew. The bees on the corner of the plant are not the full swarm, and although there are a lot of bees at the plant, I have the idea that they are a small portion of the swarm proper'.

'So the bees at the plant are a raiding party or something,

are they?' The old man looked at Andrew and saw that the question was posed in all innocence, the young man's deep green eyes shone with life and clarity. There was no hint of sarcasm or disrespect of any kind. 'You know, my young friend, I think you might be nearer the truth than you think. These bees are seriously angry and I think they are striking out, and I'm not convinced that their anger is blind'. Andrew's face was blank but thoughtful, he wasn't sure he quite understood Mr. Akaya's meaning, but he'd come to not only like this unconventional old man, but also to respect him.

The two moved along the edge of the blazing yellow field. The hedges and trees that separated the huge fields were abundantly green, branches and fronds swaying in the gentle warm breeze. 'Look at the hedges, Andrew. Tell me what you see'. The young man stopped walking and took in more consciously what was going on around him.

'Well, there's loads of birds fluttering about and diving in and out of the bushes. Umm, and there's all kinds of flying insects buzzing about. Is that what you mean?'.

'Yes, that is what I mean. Now look again and tell me what you don't see'. Andrew was momentarily puzzled, his eyes screwed up in a frown. Then, with a flash he had it. 'I can't see a single bee, Mr. Akaya. Not a one'.

'Exactly, Andrew. Where are the bees? They're not all at the plant, so where the blazes are they, hmm? And if you take a close look at the fields of rape, do you see any bees, I don't' . Andrew looked.

'No, Mr. Akaya. I can't see a one. Wasps, dragonflies, butterflies, but no bees'.

'Exactly. Come on, we've got to find the swarm, or swarms for that matter. They can't be far away'.

Akaya led the way back the way they'd came to the top of the field. When they had reached the clearing, Akaya stopped and scanned all around the area, the surrounding trees, hedges and bushes. Andrew followed suit and he too searched, although, he wasn't quite sure he knew what to look for, he'd never seen a swarm of bees before.

After a few minutes of quiet seeking, Akaya tapped Andrew's shoulder lightly. 'There they are Andrew', and he pointed to a large dark patch in a hedge that lay at the far end of the plant.

'But how do you know that that dark patch, all the way over there is the bees?'

'Because a large dark shadow in a sunlit healthy green hedge, doesn't belong there Andrew. That's why, come on'. Akaya led the way across the couple of hundred or so yards to the hedge and stopped about three feet in front of it. And sure enough, they they were. Andrew was amazed, never in his life had he seen so many bees in one place. There must be thousands of 'em, he thought. He began to feel unsettled, a little fearful. The noise of the bees was frantic, and it seemed as though his and Akaya's presence aggravated the bees further, they began to fly around the two men as they stood and watched. Andrew began swatting them, worried that he was likely to get stung. 'Don't flap about Andrew, you'll annoy them. I think they're annoyed enough, don't you? Come on'. The pair walked over to Akaya's car, and as they neared it, a young woman came running out of the office section of the building. She too had a shock of red hair that fell in waves well beyond her shoulders, and features which looked familiar. 'Andrew, Andrew, what the hell are you doing!? You'll get stung all over and you know what happens when you get stung, you're allergic to stings!'

'That's wasps Nancy, not bees. Even I know the difference. Now stop worrying and getting all unnecessary'. The young lady was up close to them now. Andrew smiled at Akaya. 'She's my sister, Mr. Akaya. It's allright'. The old man nodded knowingly and opened up the back of the old Morris. 'Besides...', Nancy went on. 'This old man's not even a proper bee keeper, and you could get stung to death. Think about it Andrew, it's not worth it for goodness sake!'

'Nanc, Mr. Akaya ain't a proper swan keeper either, but he

saved all them swans, didn't he?'. Nancy stamped her foot and turned to walk away, then stopped and turned. 'Mum'll be really annoyed if you have to go to hospital for stings, Andrew. I wouldn't want to be in your shoes, blinking fool!' And off she stamped back towards the offices. Andrew raised his eyebrows in a fond wide smile.

'You wouldn't believe she's my younger sister, would you?' Akaya smiled.

'Your sister means well, you'd be concerned if she didn't care. So if you are allergic to stings, what are you doing helping me, Andrew?'

'Like I said, Mr. Akaya, wasp stings do me serious damage, bee stings don't. Besides, when I'm working with you, I always feel safe. I know it sounds daft, but it's like I feel protected'. As they both stood there, the elder man taller than the younger, their eyes met and emerald met violet. Andrew suddenly felt a wash of immense peace wash over him, he looked at the old man and his face lit up, he began to shine. 'Whenever you help me Andrew, you are protected. Now come on then, let's go and help our angry little friends'.

Akaya picked up the large leather bag and asked Andrew to bring the toolbox and the cutting tools. As they were walking away from the car, Davis of finance came up to them accompanied by another burly man in white overalls. Andrew explained that he was the plant manager. 'Have you a plan, Mr. Akaya. Can you see a solution to the problem?', Davis asked.

'Yes indeed, Mr. Davis. And I'm expecting to be able to resolve the situation within the hour'.

'That would be great. Otherwise I'm going to have to send everyone home. Do you still need Andrew?'

'More than ever'.

'Yes, Andrew told me that he'd worked with you before'.

'Correct. The young man was a great help to me with another matter with the natural world and it's exploitation'. The two senior company men looked at each other in a sideways glance, apparently genuinely not understanding. 'Exploitation, Mr. Akaya? I'm not sure I'm with you there'.

'Not to worry gents. We'll sort it, wont we Andrew?' Akaya said brightly. Andrew nodded agreement. 'Now then gentleman, before Andrew and I start, I must ask you to keep all the staff away from us, preferably by the factory walls. And please, no sudden or frantic movements, even at that distance. We don't want to anger the bees further. Andrew!' Akaya waved his friend to follow him to the tall hedge. Andrew's mind and heart were all a'buzz, but of a very still and peaceful buzz. He recalled the time he'd helped the old man before. It was the same then, that sense of complete inner peace and stillness, despite the appalling situation they'd had to deal with. He didn't understand why or what, and he frankly didn't care. Peace, after all, he mused, is peace.

They had stopped a couple of feet away from the hedge and the turbulent bees. Their mood hadn't altered, Andrew noticed. He put the tools down and turned to look at Akaya, who was standing erect and still, the bag in his hand and gazing intently, but with a calm composure at the thick deep, dark writhing swarm. 'Now Andrew', he said quietly but firmly. 'Firstly, I think we know each other well enough now to dispense with formalities. My name is Norman, Norman Akaya. Call me Norman from now on, okay?'

'Yes, of course, er, Norman'.

'Secondly, I need you to remain calm, whatever happens. Okay?' Andrew nodded. Akaya placed the bag on the ground and picked up the shears and secateurs. 'Er, Norman?'

'What?'

'Shouldn't we be wearing those hats with the gauze in front of them, like the bee keepers wear?'

'Not necessary. Now stand and remain calm, observe and listen, especially to the bees'. Andrew wasn't too sure about that but, he trusted Norman Akaya and did as asked. He remained motionless and watched quietly. Then Akaya did something very unusual. Allowing his arms to fall gently to his sides he began to chant a long continuous note. It sounded quite beautiful, a very calming 'aaaaahhhh' sound. After a couple of minutes or so of the chanting, he noticed that the bees were actually becoming more and more quiet. They too were becoming calm. Their furious buzzing became a relaxed drone and the writhing more gently pulsing.

'Now Andrew, take the secateurs for a moment. First we have to locate the Queen'. Then with the shears in hand, Akaya gently trimmed away the branches immediately surrounding the bulk, being careful to catch the cuttings before they dropped and placed them carefully on the ground close to the hedge. Then Andrew heard a, 'Aha, there she is', and put the secateurs into the old man's outstretched hand and watched him cut out the main branch that the Queen rested upon. As soon as he did that, the tone of the buzzing rose again. Akaya began his chant once more, and once more the bees quietened down. 'Pass that bag over here please, Andrew'. Andrew did so, and watched Akaya gently remove the branch holding the queen and place it slowly into the bag. The stiffness of the leather kept the hinged top open as Akaya held it with arms outstretched. Bees rose from the hedge in great numbers knowing the queen had disappeared. Andrew began to feel a little nervous as they flew around he and the old man. Many of the bees, sensing and scenting the whereabouts of the queen, slowly began to fly in descending wild spirals into the bag. Andrew looked the old man keen in the eye. 'I don't like this Mr. Akaya, not one bit'.

'Listen to the bees Andrew, listen to the furthest and gentlest sound, all the while slowly helping me, watching them. Don't give them fear and nerves, give them calm embracing love, just like you did the swans Andrew. Instinctively and naturally'. More and more of the bees left the hedge and became a thickening cloud. And then slowly but surely, the young man found his spiritual feet. He seemed to be stepped back from his body, a place of detachment and yet wholesome, embracing, just like the old man had said. He found himself tapping into a real world of calm and stillness that lay behind and within the sounds of the bees. Mr. Akaya's eyes never left his friend, he observed and felt the change occurring. Without being asked, Andrew stepped to the hedge and reached into it, picking up the thin branches that Akaya had cut, and placed the heavily bee-laden fronds gently into the bag. The bag started to stretch slowly downward, extending itself with the weight and bulk of the bees. Andrew stepped back a pace and was able to watch and take in the whole scene. In his new found stillness his mind became as clear and calm as a clear water lake, he possessed a heightened awareness and perception. The colours were brighter, the sunshine more brilliant, everything he saw permeated by a living light. And from that light, images began to form in his mind as if upon a screen before his brow.

Before his mind's eye, fields and fields of the rolling countryside unfolded before him. Green lines of hedges criss-crossed the rape seed yellow golden landscape, a dark cloud spread and enveloped the land. The bees. The cloud dissipated, the yellow fields were more golden, more alive. The pollination. The yellow withered, the green hedges turned pale then brown and then became bare with the frost and snows of winter. The sky turned grey and the sun weak and watery, fields and fields of brown ploughed earth, snow drifted and silent in sleep. Rows and rows of white bee hives ran before his eyes like a film, thousands of them in desolate fields spread throughout the unfolding land. In the background he heard a sound, a continuous note, Akaya chanting. That same note, that continuous 'aaahhhhh' seemed to live in and arise from that encompassing light. Then a single white hive stood alone before his inner eye. The seasons changing behind and around it. All the while that chant sounded throughout. Now the bees bringing pollen, streams and streams of bees to-ing and fro-ing, carrying bulging sacks of pollen from the yellow fields. Inside the hive he saw the hanging squares of filled honeycombs, surreally the vision expanded, so that he saw hundreds upon hundreds of rows of honeycombs and as the winter came, slowly but surely the miniature warehouses of honey began to solidify. But it wasn't ice crystals he saw forming, Andrew saw that the actual honey became more and more crystalised. The bees tried to feed on the rape honey, they persisted and persisted but it was useless, their food had become as rock, inedible. The noise of the panic stricken bees rose and rose into a crescendo of pain and suffering as millions upon millions of bees began dropping dead in eventual silent starvation. And then silence pervaded all and spring came again and all he saw were piles and piles of dead bees. And then he knew the reality of the absence of the bees from the fields. The pollinated rape seed oil plants crystallised the honey, decimating the swarms. So that was what the old man meant by 'exploitation of the natural world'.

When the stream of images and sounds had ceased, Andrew saw Mr. Akaya still standing before him with the now very full bag in his still outstretched hands. Bees still buzzed around, but almost lazily so, without panic. Akaya was looking directly at him, his violet eyes radiant. 'Andrew, help me carry this to the car, please', he said quietly. Andrew took one side of the leather bag and they both slowly carried the bag across the clearing. A thin cloud of bees followed them. As they neared the car, something extraordinary happened. They bees that had grouped at the corner of the building began to remove themselves from the building as if they were one entity. The staff watching below saw a thin cloud of bees as they descended and hovered around and above Akaya and Andrew. The two men gently lifted the bag into the back of the car. Once safely stowed, Akaya turned to Andrew and asked, 'what did you see Andrew?' So Andrew told him, and when he mentioned the chanting, the old man interjected with, 'Middle C, Andrew'. Being musically untrained, it meant nothing to him. Akaya saw that, 'it's said to be the ancient note of creation', he said evenly. 'That's why the bees respond to it. Did you not hear and see that in the vision?'. Andrew nodded but said and thought nothing, merely absorbed what the old man was saying. 'Would you collect the tools up, Andrew?' The young man turned and walked over to the hedge. On his way back, Mr. Davis and his sister Nancy walked briskly over to him. 'Are you allright Andrew?, Nancy asked quickly. 'You're unharmed are you?' asked Davis.

'Yes, yes, I'm fine thanks. It all went very well, did you see?'

'Yes, but I can't believe he didn't use smoke and protective hats', Davis said.

'I can't believe you helped him without protection, Andrew. Are you sure you haven't been stung?' Nancy managed to look both worried and annoyed at the same time

'I'm positive, Nanc, now stop fretting. Truly, everything's fine'. For himself, Andrew felt as though he'd done some real good in the world, he felt alive and in harmony with life. The old man walked over to meet him. 'How would you like to help me take our little friends to their new home?'

'I'd love to Norman, but...',

'don't worry about it, I'll clear it with the clock-watcher'.

Davis had been watching and saw that Akaya was ready to leave. He approached him with a wide smile. 'I don't know or understand how you did it, Mr. Akaya, but very well done, very well done indeed. I'm not sure I can quite believe what I saw. Amazing!'. Davis shook Akaya's hand enthusiastically. 'Glad to be of service, Mr. Davis', he said warmly. 'You'll have no trouble with the bees now, I'm sure. I'm going to need help relocating the bees, may I borrow Andrew for the afternoon?'

'Yes, of course. By all means. You'll send us the bill?'

'Indeed I will. Cheerio, then'.

When he got to the car, Andrew asked, 'what are we going to do with them, then?'

'I've got two empty hives in the small orchard behind my house, Andrew. And the meadow the trees are standing in, is full of wild flowers, clover and all manner of herbs growing wildly'. The old man looked at his young friend and winked. 'Next year, we'll have free honey and happy bees Andrew lad.

Come on, let's go'. As the old Morris Minor drove away with its back doors open, Nancy, Davis and the others by the plant watched them leave and saw a thin dark cloud following them.

Transiting

When the compass pointed
            north,
            in two different directions,
            yet being in the same place,
            we were born.

As Venus traversed the
            horizon,
            and expressed two opposite
            aspects of the one, we
            came together.

After the healing fire
            had touched our hearts, flowing
            between us, and pouring
            through our eyes,
            we kissed.

When it returned to its
            source,
            renewed, purifying, having
            purified us,
            we loved.

Hearthbuilding.

Stay. Open the front door
 And I shall open the rear.
  Let us walk through
   The house
    And meet by the fire;
     The fire where magic
      Is possible,
       The fire of purification,
        The fire of truth, our truth.
         Let us build a hearth,
          Where a child may play
           Safely,

           We'll pack the coals
           With chestnuts
           And warm our wintered
           Hearts.
           We'll roast the potatoes
           Of our souls,
           Clear, clean and crisp,
           Sweet and fragrant.

           Let that which we have
           Become the jasmine of
           Our chimneys.
           Stay....

Into Flight

And in between
the folds of the night,
the sheets of your caresses
that leave your hands,
meets my hurting
and bear me up
upon the wings
of love.

Landscapes

Autumn gold, rich in splendour,
potent with promise and change;
leaves fall, stripping trees bare,
covering roads slippery
and blocking drains.
Autumn brisk, autumn cold,
lying damp, turning brown;
thinking of yesterday, hoping for
tomorrow, opposite poles united
in motion, flayed bare between sorrow
and joy; all is change, death and decay.
Even glaciers melt eventually;
out of their marches, we know our
landscapes. Autumn gold, rich in
splendour, made richer in the
undeniable pact of growth.

Silent Phone

The phone goes
down and it's silent
again;

aloneness is a lifetime
apprenticeship,
we're all trying to learn.

Another Look

I need to have some dream-time,
do you mind if I sleep alone?
I need to see the voice
that's been there, since
before I was born.

Doing The Leith walk

They all do it, it's amazing, all of them at it.
All the young posers in their colourful
hairdo's and I'm going to be different clothes.
The Hindus, the Muslims, the Spaniards, the
Italians, the Pakistanis and the Indians, the
skinheads and the hippies, the colourful
sari's, the bright jewels in pierced noses
and the skin tight black tights, saying I
dare you to pinch my bum girls, showing
off their form, driving guys wild with desire
and lust, the gays with their I don't care if
you do know I'm a poofter walk. They're
all here doing the Leith Walk. Even the drunks
that stagger lean and fall, against the stone buttresses
of the church opposite do it, yet few of them
know what it is. The ladies of the night do though.
But then the street is named after them and their
predecessors, from the days when ships docked
into Leith, like cars and taxis in Piccadilly, and the
crew leapt shore-bound with fat wallets and a bulge
in their trousers, and the sisters of mercy, the
angels of the darkness comforted their cabin
fever and woman-less weeks, sharing their
bodies with the drunken pleasure of knowing
he needs it, wants it and is willing to pay
for it. You pay for it one way or another, he said.
What's the difference between a thirty quid meal and
countless gins, and giving the lady thirty quid up front,
s'all the same ain't it? Better to be honest and have
done with it, than all the mucking abaht. And the lady
and the sailor sink into rhythmical intimacy and unison
that has made Leith Walk famous and happily
notorious. Thank God!

Night Walk: Pendine to Brook After The Breakdown

Stillness.
The vast stillness permeates this lonely night road,
Seeping through everything on it, above it
And uniting and embracing the stillness within.

The dark,
Domed cloudless sky made geometric
And hexagrammatical
By distant stars, doorways to even stranger,
More colourful realities.

Blue black
Silence, pierced by crickets, metronomes
To the soft tinkling, trickling stream, reeded,
Hedged and rosebay-willowed.

A toad,
Croaking leaps headlong in,
And beckoned, an inviting female
Brruupp replies.

Myriad fireflies,
Phosphorous lamps vying
In competition to covet
Another's lover for the night it seems.

Soft
Padding footfall, rhythmic gentle,
Keeps my languid pace in time,
Heartbeat and step, slowly vibrant,

Pulsing in life.
So,
Full moon bright and glistening,
Blanket and sheen the sea-scape,

Silhouette the windless dunes,
Past the still marshes,
Left wind-carved
Into soft feminine curves

That languish for a kiss
From the swish
of the whispering sea; expectant.
Call owl,

With your twisting, revolving head,
Flutter your heart and sing your wings,
Swooping over laid back dozing cows
To your screeching lover.

Chiffon webs,
Draped silvered on bush and herb,
Lace traps inviting the unwary'
While others hang taut,

Conjured night dew jewels,
Like women of the night,
Beautiful, dangerous
And eerie.

Caught,
In the magic of the creatures
Of the night, I stop and gaze
Into mercury streaked movement,

Of the passing flow.
Filigree petals,
Iridescent, violet pink,
Float by and pass,

Moving on
Like so many fragile lovers.

One remains caught
For a while behind smooth

Rounded stone, as if to say,
I am here, see me
in my delicate vulnerability,
scented and dampened by

life's fickleness.
Its lonely beauty touches the heart;
A sad note reverberates in mine.
Then it too

Breaks free, riding the surface
To meet a greater
Destiny.
The moon,

With its stolen light, graces,
Mocks and fools us all, deceives
Us into thinking its glow is its own.
Mind absorbs the panorama

Of loving life;
As the petal lets go, so must I.
Tomorrow,
The sun rising anew,

Brings, a fresh dawn.

Own Feet

Count the words
like matchsticks in a box.
Contain them and
send them away
into a cloud of unknowing.

No burning, no battles,
no yearning, no gains,
only the body count of
another silent war;
stillness of the slain conquers.

Running naked through wet grass,
through the flowering forests,
chasing reindeer thoughts.
Flowering fields of violet
bathe my eyes, clear.

The wish was almost real,
but snaked tongues carry
foulest deeds and poison,
spinning webs of deceit,
to carry in an empty suitcase.

Traveling light takes me
anywhere, anywhere I wish.
No theft, I'll take only
what I know. Keep yourself,
the you, you don't know.

Till sunset meets the dawn,
I'll walk, run, swim seas
of red, sands of black;
I'll tread glaciers again
and sit on peaks of gold.

Quiet, Now

Deep wishes unvoiced,
lying, defying being
wished.

The verbalised dream
left alone,

while love raises
its soft feet,
and treads across
my hopeful heart.

Rooms With A View

This room has two places,
One in my mind and the other
Where I see.

This room is in Berlin,
Czechoslovakia
And Washington D.C.

In both rooms
The shadows are the same
And the light, as I choose to give it.

In my mind, the shapes
And cadences in colour, sound
Are as I choose to live it.

In the corner in Berlin
The loneliness smells the same
As the contours and cellars in my skin.

In the attic, where the light is brightest,
The boundaries fade
Where my balls are tightest.

And it all becomes akin
To where my hearing
Becomes sightless,

And in seeing nothing,
No boredome, no same coloured walls
I hear everything

And the still sound of light
Remains;
And vision returns

While blindness rolls
Away with waves
Of all islands.

The Dream of The Swan

In the dream of the swan,
she was as the ducks
and the doves.

In the dream of the swan,
the tears in her eyes were
as the waters she swam.

The webs between her feet,
as the webs of life that
held everything together.

Her dream was of the fabric
of dust, that came from stone

borne by the mountain,

Which was as
the speck of dust
in God's eye.

In the dream of the swan,
she was all things created
and all yet to be.

The food she craned her
neck for, of herself,
her sustenance, her breath.

Silent, more sure silent
than a ticking clock, were
the waters, the weeds -

the sky, the fish,
the hook, loaded with
lead weights that choked

the self same
breath away
from her.

In her dream,
the swan,
she dreamt again.

Very Tainted Love

What chance the innocence
remaining pure?
The expected delight of life
turned sour ,
by trusted hands and tongues
so dear?

The abuse of nature's children
soon to tell,
when growing older, fumbling
finger's seeking
love, discover they cannot see
the loved one so well.

Prejudiced by unrequested
visors of fear,
the clarity spoilt, the purity
tainted
by gushing, frightened
youthful tears,

that spill into adulthood;
building chasms,
between the yearning, the desire
and the need.
Raging conflicts, creating empty
emotional spasms.

Each child, a spark of heavenly
prayers,
a three piece puzzle, father,
mother, self.
But where finds the child, beneath
parental emotional

layers? What then the chance,
what then?

Some Bother

In supplication
she kneels before me,
and I still think
in dreams chivalrous.
Can man or woman
be both human and noble?
I only know I have been
both noble, ignoble
human and beast.

I love them both
within the mind, that
sees two separate parts
as the same.
Two rivers as they become
the planetary sea, where
life as consciousness began.
Only love could be bothered
to make the effort.

Razor's edge

I don't remember asking to be lonely,
it must have happened when I wasn't looking.

Waves of change move through me, sometimes,
dragging me along reluctantly, screaming,

confused and angry at the Gods.
In solitude, reaching out and within again.

Folly and wisdom have brought me here,
and the path still unfolds before me.

Enchanting, scary; the razor's edge
between isolation and comfort.

A hand reaches out to me from the darkness,
and a heart speaks and winks to me.

The dark empty caverns of my soul
are warm again.

Inward

O secret riding upon my soul,
come hither and speak to me wise,
pour forth your pearls and teach me
that I may drown these long heard cries.
For where you come from, I must go
and trace my destiny homeward,
and surely learn to release myself
and push my heart more forward.
You speak of love and truth that is real
and I feel my spirit answer,
for, when I come to join the kill
I see, I AM the answer.

Unfettered

I looked to see illusion,
it hemmed me by the throat.
I saw no way of leaving,
I wanted just to float.
Along the river of life
to denizens only explored
by the few, I thought that
this was blissful, it was,
I grew wings and flew.

The Meaning of the Call

I'll take the isolation, the bloody battered head,
the worried determination,
and all the battle's dread.
Just give me a glimpse of meaning
and the smile of a child at play,
so that just on occasion,
I can turn and say,
your will is taken as read.

It's not that I fear the outcome,
the colourful collection of scars,
nor the loss of loved ones
who never understood the wars.
But fear of fear itself will trip me,
should I fail to watch the dawn,
then, as ever and on,
I will fight to live by your laws.

Did I tremble before your throne?
Did I not look you clean in the eye?
Even though I stood before all
and humbly swallowed my pride.

Take not these words for treason,
nor of allegiance false,
but of my reiteration,
that I will stay the course.

Then, when the sun sets finally,
I'll be glad with a smile to die.

Shades

As Prometheus, we steal from the Gods;
not fire, but time; time to be together.
Time to sit and talk and bend the evening
hours towards dawn.

Our binding rock are schedules
uncompromising; obligations unredeemable,
and the worship of the God dollar,
that steals time from us.

In the intensity of stolen moments,
we unwittingly rush into mutual discovery
and passion, and then trigger the fuse of
self-absorption, erupting like fireworks

rocketing to the heavens, colourful,
explosive and fizzling to the ground
like a half burnt carcass. Fiery joy,
reaching a peak, then falling to the damp earth.

Hearts full of love that meet,
wishing to give love; crash and
miscommunicate their intentions;
'tis then, the Gods we stole from, laugh

at our well meant errors of humanity.

In reaching out, we reached, passed and
the shared joys became blurred by the
dark shades of our lack of vision.

Shattered

I drop the bottle,
it shatters as mirrors,
like the dreams of my youth.

I put the
pieces together,
using my soul as glue,

and the dream and
the bottle are stronger
than before.

Only this time,
the bottle is filled
with a different spirit.

,

Stranger In The Park

Stranger In The Park